NO EASY FIGHTS

Eddie Newell

. ISBN 13: 9781983162572

Also from Eddie Newell.

The Kecaled Pick Me Up

A blog converted into a book. It is meandering, it is meaningless, it is there to pick up and put down whenever you need a smile. The ideal companion for the commute, holiday and lunch or coffee break.

5.0 out of 5 stars **Kecaled certainly lives up to his billing!**
17 April 2018
Kecaled has a lovely way of seeing everyday events and colouring them with a wit and charm, which is freshly engaging and comical. I dipped in and out, over a few days and enjoyed them all. I defy anyone not to see the humour and candour of 'Kecaled' - Highly recommended. MK.

5.0 out of 5 stars **Enjoy and Smile**
14 May 2018
This made me smile and found myself binge reading and seeing the lighter side to life. Enjoy. VT.

5.0 out of 5 stars **Five Stars**
4 March 2018
Fantastic read, brilliant writer and very funny, definitely worth a read. DL.

5.0 out of 5 stars **Great read**
27 May 2018
Bitesize chunks to help pull you back to the lighter side of life. Funny and relatable, this book will make you laugh and prompt funny memories. Enjoy!! CD.

Coming soon from Eddie Newell.

Justice Within

Eloise Langley has an idyllic life, loving husband & family, successful, wealthy and she has had a significant impact on healthcare. Her electronic chip implants (Chipsules) have reduced waiting times for many medical tests and the government is considering offering them free to all 5 year olds, such is their favourable feedback from medics and patients. Over 5 million people have the implants so far.

Then her eldest son is killed in a road accident, by a driver many times over the legal alcohol limit and speeding. Yet, through the combination of a technicality, daddy's money and the old boys network, the sentence the driver receives is minimal, negligible for such an offence. Eloise wants justice and she is prepared to risk her comfortable life and her liberty to achieve it.

When the time is right she hands herself into the police and informs them of a potential suspicious death and alludes to the fact she may be involved. More than that, if justice is not meted out in the manner she wants it, many more lives could perish. Those who celebrated in her Chipsule invention, could now see it used to blackmail them.

Her extravagant demands are outside of the law, but to say no could put millions of lives at risk. The case goes to the highest echelons of law enforcement and government, to see who is prepared to make a decision and either give in to her blackmail or call her bluff and possibly let loose the biggest mass murderer of our generation?

Can one woman take on the whole legal system, and the forces of government, and succeed?

Her ace card is that she knows so many people have justice within them.

PROLOGUE.

"You may not always have a comfortable life and you will not always be able to solve all of the world's problems at once but don't ever underestimate the importance you can have because history has shown us that courage can be contagious and hope can take on a life of its own." - Michelle Obama.

In every major city, or even in most communities, we all go along with our lives oblivious to how others live theirs. However weird, selfish, selfless, criminal or perverse those lives are, they happen within spitting distance every day, but we are unaware or uninterested in them. Perhaps the real truth is we are happier not knowing, even frightened to contemplate their existence, so they remain invisible and indifferent to us. We might nod at nameless people, recognise some familiar faces who are often around, but that is about the depth of most people's interest in the array of 'neighbours' we encounter daily.

Then, even fleetingly, we may find ourselves drawn into their worlds, alien worlds that do not fit our ideals, our morals and we struggle to comprehend them. When that does happen the real jungle so many of us live in reveals itself and we yearn for our bland, normal, often boring life to regain control. The food chain that we all exist within, becomes ever more obvious as the Silverbacks constantly grapple for superiority and for the power that goes with this. They exert that power on the weak and the ones who just want an easy life and so their dominance becomes established.

Donna is a very decent human being, who through choice and circumstance carries a heavy load, but she is savvy enough to know of the nastiness flourishing out there. Her reality, is having enough of a battle with day to day existence to give too much thought about what might be happening in the lives of those in this or any other community. Whether life is cruel, finds humour in misfortune or we are all taking part in a game show, with new challenges being thrown in all the time, is of no consequence when it comes our way. An uncomfortable glimpse of a life that had been hidden by a brittle facade up to this point, was heading for Donna.

Donna is a good person, the sort other people refer to as 'salt of the earth'. She does the right thing more often than not, she is a good friend and lives her life in a straightforward manner.

Russ Tomkins lost any goodness he may have had a long time ago, as he needed to be feared to run his type of business. Cross him and not only would you suffer appropriately, but as an example to others, chances are you would suffer inappropriately. He did not have friends, as he could not trust anyone. His acquaintances were only that, because they foolishly thought this afforded them some safety, some protection should they upset him down the line. His business was mercenary, and the way he maintained his business was by being merciless.

She lived frugally, and it was mostly a struggle. He lived the high life and luxuries were the norm. Evil was stalking Donna and about to strike. Could her form of goodness, hold his corrupt operation at bay when it came for her? He had money, power and an army of heavies, she had her nous, courage and a big gob.

CHAPTER 1.

"It takes many steppingstones, you know, for a man to rise. None can do it unaided." – Joe Bonanno.

Gnnnnnrrrhhh 48 gnnnnnrrrhhh 49 gnnnnnrrrhhh 50. Christ! Donna arched her back and stifled the scream she so wanted to unleash, a boxing gym was not the place for that. She finished her work out with 50 sit ups, whilst holding a weight plate to her chest. She threw this unceremoniously onto the floor. There is little point in hating inanimate objects, but even so, her dislike of that lump of iron at that precise moment was real enough. Her insides felt as though someone was squeezing and twisting them with red hot hands.

She looked up and saw the devilish grin of her coach, PD, his eyes twinkling to reveal the big kid he is. "Having fun?" He hissed. "There are times when I could gladly kick you in the balls," she laid her head back on the floor and put her hands over her face to help cope with the pain. "And take the chance of ruining our plans for children," the grin was wider now as he was pleased with his rapid response. "PD, if I had met you when you were 40 years younger and in your prime, then what can I say........it would STILL have been no." He said nothing, he loved this girl. Even when hurting, her quick mind worked like lightning to let out these put downs. He became more and more fond of her throughout the time they worked on her fitness and boxing skills and the banter they engaged in was a bonus. Not having children of his own, meant he had little to no idea of how to be any kind of father figure for her, but did she really need that anyway, as she was pretty switched on. However, he felt very protective of her and the more time they had spent together the more this grew. The fact that she was good looking could hardly escape his attention, but that was neither here nor there to him. His appreciation was of something far deeper, as this girl had a personality that was so likeable and a determination that was unshakeable, as she chased her dreams of a life much better than she had known up to this point.

The burning was starting to ease, and the sweat was now really starting to flow as her heart rate dropped and less blood was being pumped from the muscles to the skin. As heat briefly built up in her muscles, her blood temperature rose and the temperature of that same blood passing through the brain triggered more sweat. She liked this rush of perspiration as it told her body the workout was over, and this was the storm before the welcome calm of cooling down.

Her body ached all over, the sort of ache she had known for so long and weirdly had started to enjoy. Forget all that no pain, no gain stuff of the movies or what January gym goers told themselves to keep motivated after 15 minutes of mild exercise, she knew she was fit and that unless it hurt she was not making those tiny steps that kept increasing her fitness, stamina and just as importantly in her sport, a resistance to pain.

She rolled on to one side and pulled herself up into a sitting position. PD had moved away and was chatting to a couple of the younger lads, offering insight into their technique with his usual, 'let me show you, now you try' style and as ever a grin and quip were never far away. He poked out a couple of jabs into the shadows, dipped his head down and then released an uppercut to demonstrate what he wanted them to practice. He relaxed his stance and pointed to one of them at about mid chest height. As the boy looked down, PD lifted his hand to catch him gently on the nose. The boy flew his head back at the unexpected contact and all three laughed at the silly prank. PD sauntered off to play somewhere else.

Her post workout recovery was advanced enough for a smile to emerge. It was half about what he was doing and also about the pride she felt in this silly old man and the gym he ran. Where would all these young lads and girls be and what would they be doing without PD's boxing clan? They did not give him any lip, well nothing malicious, as he somehow commanded respect without even trying as he was the coach, an ex pro fighter and in this gym, he was 'the man'. If, however, anyone did upset PD, they soon felt the heat from the senior fighters who would walk through walls for him. The young fighters enjoyed being a part of this little community and mixing with the heavyweights, the better known boxers and of course the ex-boxers, promoters and other sorts who liked hanging around the tough, macho world of a fighting gym. The ex-boxers were a mixture of success and failure in life and whilst none had gone on to national acclaim in the fight game, locally a few had done alright with some good wins at minor pro meets. After that, some had got good jobs and the majority had settled for a more basic lifestyle, whilst others felt they could and should have done better as a fighter and became angry at the world; they had not been promoted properly, been given the wrong fights at the wrong times or any number of reasons that did not reflect on any lack of ability on their behalf. Normal jobs were not for them and yet as they could not get the jobs they felt matched their status, many did not work and returned to the gym to remain part of this family, this tribe that had been such a big and comfortable part of their life. The whiff of beer breath hung around them and acted as a constant reminder of the only coping strategy they knew. Of course, it was a self-defeating approach that was only feeding their anger and despair, but it was also a well-trodden road for once proud young men who felt somehow wronged or unfulfilled. Once they took that path, turning back was the hardest fight they'd ever had or have.

In their minds they were a source of motivation for this young new breed, by passing on their experience, their expertise and just being around had to be a boost for the youths. The reality was somewhat different. The current intake did not always know who they were and whilst they acted respectfully, as PD instilled in them to do, the main motivation these washed up fighters provided, was a resolve to not finish up like them.

Donna had her plan and she would stick to it; carry on working in her job at the local supermarket whilst she pursued her boxing dreams. If it worked out well and she made some decent dough then brill, invest it wisely and consider whatever options she had at that stage. If, however, success became ever more a dream and less a potential reality, she would jack it in, find something else that paid more than stacking shelves and that would let the kids have the life they deserved, really deserved. Boxing had to be contained as a means to an end and nothing more, but whilst it continued to have the potential to get her to where she wanted to be financially, she would stick with it and as soon as that was no longer the case, she would move on.

She liked being really fit, which had developed into something of a drug as she worked so hard to sustain peak performance levels. Equally, there is the hope the fight game gives, of a better life through the financial riches on offer to the elite. On the down side, Donna knew the clock was ticking on how long she could wait to see if that money was ever going to be there for her. She needed to have a way to provide a proper upbringing for those kids and she could not let herself get too engrossed in the game, because at any point she may have to decide it was not to be and move on. For some, the fight game is a way of life and everything has to revolve around it, but she could not have the emotional indulgence to think like that, so she kept the relationship at arm's length. Sure, she moved things about to accommodate training and fights, but it was a business association and she knew better than to fall in love with it. Anyway, the 'living' was made by someone trying to knock your head off your shoulders every time you climbed through those ropes. Playing Russian Roulette as a job, is not the wisest thing for a mother of two. It was a love hate kinship for her; she loved being part of something she was adept at, and that had the potential to make money a non-concern, but the very nature of the sport meant, she hated, that she loved it at all.

* * *

(Danger) Russ Tomkins was the kingpin of the underworld in this locality and his two sons, Dean and Rich, could not really grasp what exactly this would tell Russ about them that he did not already know, but if the old man wanted to 'test' them then so be it. They had to come up with a way of making a tidy sum of money, without his direction, as a way of showing they were capable of taking the reins, ready for when he decided to put himself out to pasture. They merely did what they had been told up to this point, never really considering him letting go in the foreseeable future, but of late he had been dropping the odd hint and out of the blue this challenge to them. They knew how the business ran, having worked closely with him for a while, but with the prospect of taking over the firm seeming more of a reality, they had to deliver.

Rich had watched a documentary on TV about rigged boxing matches at World level and realised this could be the way for them to show Russ they were inventive and lucrative in their thinking. Dean was an avid follower of boxing and immediately saw the potential, so they agreed that was the blueprint. Dean contacted a few of the local promoters, making out he was thinking of putting some cash into a good prospect. Out of that Donna's name had been mentioned as women's boxing was on the rise and he could get a good return on his stake. He told Rich, who was sold; the sport was gaining interest and yet it was not well enough known for people to sniff out anything dodgy going on. Perfect.

They would put her in against some patsy, bet heavily against her, and make a killing as the odds were sure to be favourable. No doubt this bird would kick off, but who cares? She either played her part or she got leaned on like all the other losers they came across who needed some persuading. If a few punters did suss out what was going on, they would hand out a couple of slaps and it would all blow over.

It might have been coming sooner than they expected, but in their mind's, they would take over at some point, so was all this crap really necessary? They would play along, make a fist of it and in the meantime carry on as they were, until he actually moved aside. Life as a son of Danger-Russ was not too bad at all. No 9 to 5 shite, money aplenty and a laid-back lifestyle they both enjoyed. As Russ insisted on doing most of the running of the business, it was not unusual for them to have nothing to do. To cope with the boredom, they regularly attended a swank new gym, situated nearby, and of course chased as much skirt as they possibly could. Dean was aware of the impact his younger sibling had on the fairer sex and Rich did little to hide it. Just last night in that club, he had spotted two Oriental looking girls and both agreed they were tidy. "Rich, shall we try our luck? You can have first choice if you like." Rich grinned at him. "Why choose. I can have them both."

CHAPTER 2.

"While we try to teach our children all about life, our children teach us what life is all about." – Richard L Evans.

Despite cooling down and having a chat with a few of the guys before she left, the sweat was still flowing as Donna walked home. PD had always said she could shower at the gym, but as there was only one set of showers that meant a lot of faff in keeping everyone out whilst the 'princess' got special treatment; she was having none of that. She was determined to be an example to other girls who joined the gym, in this and many other ways, so until such a time as they had their own changing room, which based on PDs financial situation that was likely to be never, she would shower at home. She was also aware that a testosterone filled environment, such as a boxing gym, was not a place for distractions of the flesh and the second they made it aware a girl was going for a shower, then thoughts would drift. She liked being one of PDs 'lads' and she had no intention of doing anything to change that status. To avoid unnecessary fuss, she kept her straight, dark brown hair at shoulder length and had it cut so she could quickly tie it up in a ponytail. Her skin was very pale as she had no chance of getting any sun, other than when she was on a run and usually that was in a hoodie to generate heat and encourage a loss of water. Part of her unwritten remit was to make sure none of the girls who came into the gym were pretentious in any way, shape or form. *Work harder than the boys, focus on fitness and skills whilst you are in this place. If a little bit of sweat is not to your liking, then go take up something else. Think not of yourself as a girl once you walk through that door, you are a boxer. As you will find out, that is more than enough pain for everyone, so do not add to it by being one.*

The protective arm she felt round her from all the guys at the gym was such a welcome feeling. Being 'mum' to Sam and Maggie was tiring, and sometimes she felt lonely, so to have that many people care for her was overwhelming. Physically she was drained more often than not, because she was either at the gym, working at the supermarket or chasing round after two young kids. However, all of these were her choices. Mentally, she coped pretty well most of the time, but every so often she became frazzled, as the emotional and financial pressures were huge.

When Helen, her older sister, died in a car accident, Donna had decided the best life for those kids was to be with her and overnight she had grown up. There was no father on the scene, as he had disappeared after Sam was born, and there was no life insurance pay out as the premiums were too much of a luxury for people such as them. So, she made the decision to take them on with all the tears, tantrums, pressure to be a good 'parent' and other head crushing baggage that comes with being a mother. Without doubt, it was the best decision she had ever made.

In the back of her mind she knew she had never really grieved for her sister as events took hold straight away and the needs of the kids overtook everything else. She felt bad about this, because they were close and she had never said goodbye properly. The sudden nature of Helen's death had not allowed for any final words or a long hug, but at some point she was going to have to face up to the niggle in her head that told her there was a grieving process that would not go away until it was given the respect, and time, it quietly demanded. It bubbled away like a volcano gaining strength for a big blow. Before the accident they had been normal, loving, squabbling, sometimes jealous sisters, who perhaps had not shown each other too much emotion. Whereas now, she never let a loved one leave without a hug, just in case.

Medical professionals and the social workers, who made sure she was capable of looking after two other human beings, all told her the grief would come out. She accepted this, but life had just been too busy for anything as selfish as that. She knew they were right and that somewhere down the line she was heading for some dark times.

Helen would have wanted the kids to be with family and that gave her the strength to carry on at those times when it seemed all too much. The mental impact of losing Helen had affected Donna in so many ways and during those restless nights she wondered if they should have been more open about their feelings. The love was there, but it was largely unspoken and obscure. However, considering their upbringing with a cold mother, who probably viewed her kids as getting in the way of the life she wanted, and a dad who was locked up, on the run or getting into a scrape of one sort or another, then perhaps they had come through it pretty well. Mum had used some force to keep them in line, but there were no meaningful hidings, thank heavens. Dad got his anger out on men who dared to cross him, or even came close to that, so for all their failings, their parents had not exposed them to the horrors of violence on them or each other.

Tenderness, affection and what many would consider to be a normal part of a parent to child relationship was seldom in evidence. Donna was making sure her home had plenty of all of those.

Maggie was a well-adjusted nine year old, all things taken into consideration, and was doing well at school; she was bright, well behaved and liked by teachers and pupils. She had a maturity beyond her years, as it seems many who suffer a loss early in life tend to have. It's not any form of compensation, unfortunately it is nothing more than a cruel fact. Sam, seven, was coping less well and had gotten into a few fights at school as the bullies saw an easy target. The spiteful name calling and like was terrible and possibly to be expected from young kids. But how the parents could stick up for their children and turn a deaf ear to what was being said when the school had contacted them, was beyond belief. Of course, this was the real problem. Donna might not be their real mum, but she aspired to be the parent many of these idiots would never be and that gave her a calming satisfaction that kept her simmering temper under control. She would find the money for Sam to take Karate lessons or she would get him involved at the gym and then when these parents did not like their precious little babies coming home with a split lip, she would shrug her shoulders and grin. She was grinning now at the thought of it.

This was not how she had planned things, but since the drunk driver had robbed her of Helen it had instantly become her life. The police were all very nice when they knocked at her door on that haze of a day, but they were simply doing their job and breaking the news. It had been quick and painless apparently, and the bastard who had hit her was locked up for manslaughter for a long stretch, which the professionals told her should make her feel better as justice had been done. It did not. During the day in court she heard about his own problems that had led him to the demon drink and yes, she was still angry with him, but she understood a bit more. It was his day off and his boss more or less said come in now or do not come in again. As he was ashamed of how bad his drinking had become since his wife left, he could not own up to that being the reason for not turning in to do the extra shift. He should not have drunk so much, he certainly should not have driven, and his boss should not have been such an uncaring git. In the end, so what? Helen was dead. He was locked up and suffering in all sorts of ways, because he seemed an otherwise decent bloke and now had to come to terms with killing someone, to add to all his other woes. This was a lonely man, living an existence rather than a life and nothing summed this up more than when no-one from his employers turned up to court as even a token of support. She began hating him and ended up pitying him.

Her mother had told her that to take on the kids would be to throw her own life away and they should be taken into care. She had hardly spoken to her mother since then and when she did she felt totally indifferent towards her. If it had been that she was genuinely thinking of Donna, that might have been different, but as she never once offered to take the kids on herself, this seemed unlikely. A more probable explanation was, she did not want the hassle in her life or to suffer the guilt of seeing Donna giving up so much to keep them 'with family'. Some people may say the sacrifice she was making was massive, as she was still in her teens when Helen died and starting to think about a career having recently left full time education. Sacrifice my arse, she just could not let Maggie and Sam fend for themselves. Anyway, what they had given her in love and laughs more than compensated for any stupid hamster wheel career.

The flat was not great, and the kids did not have everything they wanted, but she did the best she could for them and they were more of a family than many around them. They were close, they were loving, they were a tight unit and she was proud of that. She remembered so vividly when Helen had made her understated announcement that she was pregnant and that means, 'You Donna, have a ridiculously important job as you will be an aunty.' It made her feel proud and that feeling was a constant for all the time Helen was with the kids. That was then, but now she was a hands-on, aunty-cum-mum and no matter how hard things were, she loved Maggie and Sam so much and that would see her through exactly the same as any other parent.

Donna had always been quite fit and good at sports in school but had never found one she excelled at. That might have been in part to the useless PE teachers, who did not do any more than pass on the basics of the sports she tried; athletics, netball, hockey etc. However, although she was good, she was never likely to be great at any of them. Then in her mid-teens, one of the lads she was keen on had been into boxing and he happened to train at PD's. He mentioned they did fitness as well as boxing and the first session was free if she wanted to come. Not over thinking it, as she mainly wanted to be near him for as much of the time as she could, she went along. The circuits on the bag, speedball, shadow boxing and then cardio, strength and abs exercises, straight away hooked her. She was very nearly sick the first time, which was not going to help the impression she was attempting to create for her Mr. Wonderful, but quickly she realised how much fitter she was feeling having signed up for twice weekly sessions.

PD noticed her, because she knew how to throw a punch and she went through the pain barrier without any fuss or fanfare. Most boys who came into the gym had some understanding of how to punch, as that was a male thing and dads would pass on their experience the first time their son came home a bit upset from school. *Next time, hit him on the nose like this.......* and all that making of a man stuff. Girls however, often needed more coaching as they punched more like a slap and they could hurt themselves depending on how they connected with the heavy bag. Not so Donna. She generated force from her hips as she turned them in tune with her arms. She raised her shoulders as she threw a punch and she did not telegraph when a punch was about to be thrown. Donna was quick and effective. OK, so the use of the feet was rubbish and she was too straight legged, but she was ahead of the game. He spoke to her after she had been at the gym for a few weeks and asked where she had learned how to box;

"Not sure what you mean, learned to box?"
"Well, how did you know how to hold your hands and to make good use of your shoulders and hips?"
"I watched your boxers and copied them."
"Well, I'm impressed. Fancy a go in the ring next time you come, or are you worried

you might smudge your make up?"
"Were you worried about that when you started then?"

He was just about to call her a cheeky little beggar, when she continued;
"Yeah, I would love a go and I will make sure I am make up free. That OK?"

That next week, he suited himself up with hand mitts and an old body protector and asked Donna to try and hit him. For a minute or so, he easily blocked her punches with the mitts and every so often cuffed her on the head as a little piece of motivation. Then she stepped back;

"Can I watch someone before we have another go please?" It was asked as a question, but delivered as a statement, because she was walking back to her corner and bopped down through the ropes. He was stunned for a few seconds. Then he looked all around in a slow, deliberate way. "This is still my gym isn't it?" he pointedly asked her from the centre of the ring having completed his mocking 'check' on his surroundings. She saluted him by way of confirmation and said nothing. She is some piece of work, this one. He called Kevin over, he was a decent prospect and a skilled pugilist; it will be interesting to see how much of what she sees she then utilises. He sparred with Kevin for a round and every so often he looked over at Donna. She was totally engrossed in what Kevin was doing and watched him intently. As the 3 minutes ended he saw her shadow boxing her moves and was intrigued that her feet were now far more in time with the rest of her body.

She got back in and he called her to him;

"Anything else I can do for you before we continue?" The sarcasm was difficult to miss.
"Yeah, put your gumshield in for me, like you do for him, as I think you might need it." He looked at her and grinned. He would give it a few seconds and then grant her a more meaningful tap on the head to keep her gob in check.

This time however, it was far less easy to keep her away from him as she had seen how to dummy and was using Kevin's tutelage, through observation, to good effect. She rattled the body protector on the left side of his stomach and instantly dodged out. He felt the power of her punch, "Good. Now try to hit me twice." She did not manage it, but she really went for a couple of big punches to test his gumshield out, as promised. PD used all his experience to keep just out of reach, but he was full of admiration for how rapidly she had absorbed and put in place the skills she had seen Kevin use.

He started to work with her on technique and her progression was whirlwind, so they discussed whether she should think about a real fight. She was not sure as this was still all new to her, so PD pulled a master stroke. He knew of a good female boxer who lived quite local and he was on friendly terms with her manager. He made contact and asked her to spar with Donna. Headgear on, gumshields in, heavier than normal gloves worn to take some heat off the punches and under instructions to not kill each other, the two girls sparred for three rounds. Donna had been very calm ahead of the session and PD was concerned she might freeze as she was so laid back. He had no need to worry. She got caught a few times and there was a difference in class, which was to be expected from a seasoned boxer against a relative novice, and early on it was one sided. However, as the rounds proceeded, Donna got better. She connected with a couple of tidy body shots that caused her opponent to wrap her up in a clinch whilst she let the discomfort subside. At the end on points there was only one winner, but Donna had done well. After sparring the two girls had a long chat about the fight game and then parted on excellent terms, swapping numbers and agreeing to keep in touch.

PD caught up with her after the other girl had left.

"How was that for you?"
"It was alright. Did I do OK?"
"Considering you were in with a boxer with many fights under her belt, you did pretty well. I was impressed she didn't land any big punches on you."
"Are you kidding? I saw stars for most of the first round and she winded me in the second. I was hoping to do better than that."
"You didn't seem hurt."
"No way was I going to let her know it."

The three rounds and the chat after with a fellow boxing 'sister' had intrigued Donna enough to see how good she could be at this. PD was happy at how his ploy had turned out and they worked on a plan to get her fight ready. That was the beginning, now look at her.

* * *

Maggie could not sleep and she thought she heard Sam fidgeting in his bed, so she crept across to see him.
"You OK?"
"Guess so."
"What's up little man, not like you to miss your sleep?"
"Do you remember mum? Do you think of her much?"
"Yeah, of course. She was great."
"Tell me about her."
"Oh, you remember, she was pretty, clever and she loved you very much."
"Loved us; US, very much."

"Yeah, loved US!"
"How come she was picked to die; some kids at school keep saying she must have been a really bad person?"
"Then they are idiots, so do not let it get to you. Aunty Donna says stuff happens that we can't understand that's all. Bit like you and fractions......."
(a puzzled look on Sam's face is followed by a grin)
"Night Mags."
"Night Sammy, you da man!"
"I miss mum."
"Me too. Hands up, ready for the Wilbraham Waggle?"
"Always ready."

With that they carried out their secret greeting; double handed fist bump, open palm slap and then back of the hand slap, at which point Maggie jumped up and ran to her room with hands aloft, as if she had won a sports contest.

CHAPTER 3.

"There's no such thing as good money or bad money. There's just money." – Lucky Luciano.

PD stood for 'punch drunk', with the occasional slurring of speech and shuffling walk giving this so-called nickname some resonance. Yes, he would have been wiser to have sidestepped a few of the young guns as his career headed towards its final death throes and perhaps his faculties would be more complete and intact, but he loved the game. Back then he just wanted to carry on, so considerations about his future health were in terms of a priority, non-existent. Just being known as a boxer gave him a real buzz, probably in the same way as when other occupations introduce themselves as doctors, teachers or in the army. He said it with pride every time and all the gym work, the comradery heightened by the risk they were all taking, the early morning runs in wind, rain, sleet or shine were all a necessary and, to a greater or lesser degree, enjoyable parts of that life. However, the fight itself was the real drug.

As soon as the fight was announced the attention and adulation began and it became the only topic of conversation anyone had with him.
How are you feeling?
You will murder him.
This guy was made for you.
Who will you fight next?
On and on it went. The spotlight was on him and even though he was never the headline bout, the focus on him meant it felt like he was fighting for a belt of real significance. The intensity gradually built up to the big night and then of course reached a crescendo at the fight itself. In the dressing room there were plenty of visitors offering last minute advice, back slapping, rugged good luck wishes based on causing as much destruction as possible to your opponent and sometimes even the local press had run articles or wanted a last minute comment. He loved it. He had found something he was good at, that gained him real respect from other men, interest from women and that also earned him a few extra quid.

It was a harsh, hard sport in and out of the ring. He had won fights and then faced a mob of angry supporters of his bruised combatant, who did not much like his expression of greater skills. Perhaps the discarded betting slips provided a greater insight into their fury. He would have stood up to any of them, but 10, 20, 30 or more fists coming your way, some loaded with bottles or worse, was hard to compete with. He had also suffered a few beatings from a better pugilist. When he came across them he quickly realised with such a gap in class, there was no amount of bag work or rounds of sparring that was going to close the gulf. They were impossible to hit and by the time he had begun launching an uppercut, his face and body were hit repeatedly, and hit hard. He was a decent fighter at his level and that was the sum of it.

Once he finally gave in to his ageing body, and recognised the defeats were more frequent and the recovery time longer and longer, he had to decide what next? A job working for some little shit who wanted to demonstrate his pathetic power over those in his charge was not for him. He helped at the gym for a while, just cleaning and odd jobbing around the place, until the then coach decided he'd had enough. PD was offered the chance to take over the tenancy and jumped at it. It had taken all his savings to keep the place running at times, but then he would come across a decent young lad and by acting as his manager, he got to bring in some extra money to the coffers. Either the lad fizzled out or he got a better offer from a manager more connected in the game and that was that; he wished him well and both moved on. In the meantime, PD kept the landlord happy by paying the rent each month; somehow. When a new kid joined the gym, he had a saying he used over and over;

"You might think you are the new Rocky, but the only thing rocky here is the finances, so make sure you pay your subscriptions."

His dark skin was lighter than when he was younger, probably due to his metabolism slowing down, but despite his advancing years he was pleased it had not lost all its elasticity. The short, wiry hair was now controlled by a grey majority stakeholder, but that did not matter, as it was mostly covered by his dark blue, woollen beanie. The hat had seen better days, but as it had been given to him on his last milestone birthday by the gym members, it meant a lot to him. The exact age it represented a celebration of, he chose to forget. Some wag had painted 'PD' on it in bright red a while ago and whilst he was annoyed at first, for the desecration of his prized property, he had come to love the enhancement. His teeth were yellowing and hardly straight, but they were mostly his, albeit with the help of many fillings and the odd crown. He wore specs to read, the cheapest pair he could find as he did not indulge himself that way. Facially, his previous career was not so obvious and having small ears had saved him the sufferance of cauliflowers on the sides of his head. He ate as healthy as he could afford to and avoided sugary treats or processed foods as much as possible. Still he carried a little pot belly with him and his pecs were less taut than in his heyday. The ageing process did its damnedest to remind him that was a fight no-one wins. His one guilty pleasure was a few tins of beer at the weekend, of whatever brand was on sale. It calmed him and helped him to unwind.

The ever present, plain, baggy jogging bottoms were coloured green, blue or black as he got a 3 for 2 offer some time back. He wore white vests, mostly covered by a grey, half zip fleece with the sleeves always pulled up to reveal a Muhammad Ali tattoo on his right forearm. It was faded now, sadly much less distinct than when he had it inked on forty odd years ago, but having the greatest ever boxer on his arm was still magical. At times when he needed motivation, inspiration or just a bit of moral support he placed his left hand on Ali and immediately felt better. He chose the best tattoo artist he knew of and asked for an intricate portrait of the great man's face; it was some of the best money he had ever spent.

Donna was possibly going to be his next decent pay day, but with her it was more than about the money. This girl needed a hand up in life and she was brilliant, simply brilliant to have around the gym and around him. The excitement of seeing her develop her skills kept on and on reaffirming his belief in how good she could be. It was taking years off him. She was such a fantastic learner and soaked up everything he told her. The difference he noticed between her and many of the better lads he had worked with was that she did not carry any of that macho crap with her. While they could never resist the temptation to try and knock someone's head off, she coldly and methodically destroyed her opponents. She avoided their tentative lunges and jabbing paws with apparent ease and then snap, a piercing fist landed with precision. Even when she did get caught with a heavy blow, she showed no pain, and this is very demoralising for an adversary, not to mention strength sapping. The mind is many times more powerful than the body and she instinctively knew it, along with so much more of the fight game that came naturally to her. That was what persuaded him to invest so much time and effort into her. She was tough, a 'natural' and determined; quite a combination for anyone who steps through the ropes of a boxing ring.

She did not mention her father very much, although PD knew of him, but she had said;

"My dad did not give me and my sister very much, but he did tell us this when we were being targeted by some kids down our road.

Pain is all in the mind, not your body. Forget the pain now and show no sign of being hurt. Your time to make sure they remember what they did will come down the line. That was when I learnt to control my pain and the words and odd punch or kick just seemed to bounce off us without any effect. The crap they were giving us did stop, but mostly I think that was because he threatened the dads, however the lesson stuck with me. The 'down the line' bit, was all about him, as he never forgot or forgave. Me, I cannot waste a second on some bully."

PD was a realist, his health was deteriorating and who cares if that was boxing related or not, the fact was he was on a slippery slope there was no coming back from. It was not terminal in the short term, but his ability to control his body was slowly being taken away from him. Stuff the money his managing her fights might bring, nice though it would be, more important to him was he wanted to know he had made a difference. He had a hankering to look back as he sat in his favourite care home chair and be able to feel warm with pride that he was a part of something. He had a couple of decent lads who might just fulfil their potential and get to a level none of his other boxers had managed and he was giving them the support, coaching and guidance they needed to get there. Trouble was, he had seen it all before as their immaturity got the better of them. They had got injured, or in trouble with the law, through a fight in a local pub after being goaded.

Some got distracted by the girlfriend who could not understand why they would want to spend so many hours in a gym when they could be with her. Of course, some just fell in with a few wrong 'uns. It had damaged his ability to believe in their prospects to a point where he too often had a real struggle to motivate himself to put in the ring time with them. The doubts trickled in whenever he heard 'new girlfriend' or the name of a local pub they were going to he knew could spell trouble. He talked to them, a word to the wise, but listening to him or an attractive girl was a no brainer, which he did not like, but totally understood. If only they could see he would still be in their corner in months and years to come, whereas many of those girls would be long gone. Yep, even those who were the loves of their life, 'the one' and settling down material.

It was difficult for those girls too, as these lads were at work or in education and then put in many hours at the gym. All that combined, often did not leave enough time for getting to know each other. Plus, the serious fighters would be careful what they eat and drink, how late they were out and complying with the strict regime of a boxer's life, that to someone who does not understand it only spells out boring. What was the point of a fit boyfriend if you never went anywhere decent with him? He grinned; been there, done that. Always easier to tell others than live by those principles yourself.

Someone famous had said *youth is wasted on the young* and how right they were. His certainly had been.

Donna was different. Every bit as talented as any lad he had worked with and disciplined beyond belief. She had major distractions in her life, with bringing up the kids, and in comparison, the 'lad' distractions were mostly frivolous, but she just dealt with it all and carried on. Women seemed to have that quality; if they were ill the meals still needed making, if the father of their child moved on they still had to bring the child up and the list goes on. Donna had that quality in abundance. Boxing was a way to release the tension and any anger she might feel at the world, but this was so much more than a way of getting rid of aggression for her. She had talent, she applied herself and every punch, every sit up, every round spent sparring, was driven by her craving to give Maggie and Sam the life they deserved.

PD harnessed that inner cyclone and fuelled it on the few occasions when she faltered or began letting fatigue get the better of her. He did so without any regret or uneasiness. "Are you going to give up now when two kids are at home relying on you?" This had been used and others, but it had worked as the eyes burned a little more, the punches were more intense, and she continued to stride towards her goal. On those seldom occasions where he had purposely irritated her to delve deeper into her physical and mental resources, she had left immediately after training without a word. He had not even been treated to one of her withering stares as she departed. She marched out slamming the gym door nearly off its hinges and then next day at training she punched his arm playfully and said, "Bring it on again tonight old man and let's hope I do not miss the bag and catch you," Father daughter stuff, was how he saw it.

His wooden chair, with its worn, leather effect seat had a prime position, where he could watch most of the gym from. It was rare that he sat down for any length of time as something would catch his attention and he would semi shuffle to where he was needed. From a distance he could see if the heavy bag was being clouted in a way that could damage the lad or girl attacking it or if the sparring was no longer being undertaken in a controlled manner. Despite his physical drawbacks, his speed to get to places in all corners of the gym before any permanent damage was done was down to experience.

He loved this place. OK so the walls had not been treated to a new coat of brilliant white for a while and the damp and condensation had stopped fighting each other. Their coalition had meant there were black patches all over, with streaking water marks flowing down many walls. To him it was artistic, as opposed to grim. He used it to good effect and would often call out above the grunts, the squeaking of new trainers on the floor and the general din of energy being expended;
"The walls are the only thing allowed to cry in this place, so suck it up."
"Look hard and you will see the face of a great fighter looking down on you from that wall. Can you see him? Can you make out his face, his eyes? Well, I pray he can't see you if that is what you call training."

Not all the lights worked, and he could do with some new gloves, bags and headgear, but this was a little community, a place for his 'family' of sorts to meet. There were pristine, well equipped physical havens appearing all around them as the businessmen saw a good return. Yet people still flocked to him and his old, weathered building. What he offered was a feeling of belonging and the promise, faint or not, of a career in a lucrative if intensely tough business, driven by a mentor who cared and really knew his art.

He still had some contacts in the game and they sent him fight posters or other items they would just throw away, but knew he could make good use of. The newness of the posters contrasted with most of the gym and PD used them effectively. The fights they advertised were for heroes of those he trained and many a time he walked someone over to the poster and said,

"How much do you want to make it in this game?" As the boy was about to reveal it would *'mean everything to me'*, PD would say,
"Do you think he got to fight in a huge match like that by being a lazy arse?" Again, the boy was about to offer a response when PD carried on,
"That's right, no he did not. Now if you want to be him, be in a monster of a fight like this and of course most importantly, get airbrushed for your own poster, give...me...some...effort." The awkwardness of the minor feeling of tension was released with a playful headlock.
"It'll have to be a big budget fight if they intend to make you look half decent on a poster." He let go. "You have got talent, but talent isn't enough in this business, because you will tire by the third round and be a sitting duck. You have got to work harder and get much fitter."

* * *

He turned the lights off, just like he did at the end of every day, and shadow boxed as he went, dodging a couple of imaginary punches and heavily rattling the speedball with a destructive straight right. The swagger told its own story, he still had it. The lights dimmed, but his pride did not. He used the same closing words he had been using for years and to not do so would leave him with a niggling feeling like he had left the door unlocked.

"It might not be the law of the land, but for me Queensbury rules. Thanks for the ride Mr. Ring, long may it continue."

A feeling of inner contentment coursed through him and then, and only then, could he throw his tiny empire into darkness as he headed for the exit. Between the light switch and the door, he tripped on something, but managed to keep his balance; just. Like we all do, once his balance was restored, he looked around to see if anyone had witnessed his misdemeanour and of course no-one had. He grinned at his stupidity in tripping and then at his vanity for checking who might have witnessed the trip. Then he threw a couple more punches from the door at some pretend opponent. As he closed the door he mumbled under his breath "What the fuck did I trip on anyway...."

* * *

Russ Tomkins was proud to have all the trappings of a successful man; big house in a sought-after location, large Merc with his personalised number plate, D4NGER, and tailor-made suits, to name but a few. The double breasted, wide pinstripe suits came in Gentleman Grey, Charcoal and for special occasions he donned a surprising Royal Blue to grab people's attention. He wore these with garishly coloured shirts and expensive ties that had matching pocket squares.

He enjoyed flaunting his affluence. Why not? He had worked hard at his business and given more than a pound of flesh in his personal life by making those sacrifices needed to keep him on top of his chosen profession. He was a hood, a gangster or whatever you liked to call his kind, but if there was money in it he did not care how legal it was. People fear him, and he liked that as it made running his type of business so much easier. His hired muscle is not to be messed with and every so often he would make sure they remind the street crooks and low life's who the guvnor is. It was tough who took the pasting as they might just be unlucky or perhaps step out of line at the wrong time, but that was unimportant to him. He needed to make sure everyone knew their place and did not consider stepping out of line. The odd broken bone or smashed up face was a good way to remind everyone who the king of this jungle is. The local plod knew his legal back up was impressive and seldom bothered to take him on. They had lost often enough to not want the hassle or egg on face that the press enjoyed indulging in.

However, he was getting older and even if he made running his firm look like it was dead easy, doing so was taking a heavy toll. He wanted to get out and spend some more of his fortune at an age where he could still enjoy it and perhaps find someone special to enjoy it with. He missed true female companionship, but that was not something anyone would know; like most feelings, he kept it buried out of sight, out of sound and out of mind. As he got further into the mire, the boys' mother could not stand the lifestyle and despite their love still being passionate and true, she had left him many years ago. She moved on with a good settlement and the knowledge that if she attempted to harm him or the business in any way, the repercussions would be dire. He felt a weird sense of pride that he could say that and mean it to someone he cared for so much, so he told everyone he could. He knew it would add to his already notorious reputation. As a full-on crime boss, a woman in his life would have been a weakness, not to mention a distraction, so he made the decision to forego affection and get intimacy as he needed it, pay for it if necessary. It had hardened him even more. Now perhaps, with the boys looking to take his place for more of the time, he could find a loving relationship with a lucky lady and experience that part of being a man he had intentionally locked away, somewhere deep inside him, a long time ago.

As his wealth and influence had grown so had his vanity and nothing gave this away more than his jet black hair, slicked back tight to his head, and held in place by copious amounts of a product his hairdresser recommended. He went for a wash, cut & dye regularly, believing no stray grey hairs would protect the secret of his age defying locks. It did not. The dye men use never seems to look even remotely natural, but that doesn't stop the likes of Russ swallowing the crap they put on the packaging, hook, line and sinker. Part of his stay youthful regime was to use moisturiser every day, but he didn't tell anyone as it seemed a bit out of kilter with his desired image. The balance between looking good and remaining hard in people's eyes was an everyday challenge for him. His handmade tan brogues complemented his suits, but the Superman belt buckle belied his styling and represented more his ego. To him it all added up to something special for anyone he came across, but most felt his money could be better spent on some up to date sartorial advice. He'd had a chat recently with some posh dentist in the city about having his Veneers done and had been told to allow £500 to £1000 per tooth. For the effect it would have on his appearance, he was more than happy with that and just needed to sort out the several appointments it would apparently take.

As part of handing over the business to his boys, he needed to know they were up to it. Theirs had been a very different upbringing to his and he was concerned the comfortable surroundings they had been raised in might have made them too soft for some of the difficult decisions they would have to make. Putting the frighteners on someone was nothing and the hired help would take care of that, but if that did not do the job and further action was required, that took real balls. People recovered from a slap, but doing real damage to someone or even making them disappear, that was not a step to be taken lightly. He knew, as he carried the burden of all such contracts he had put out there.

Rich and Dean were good boys who he had schooled in the ways of his business and whilst they knew the score, it was different knowing what to do and actually carrying it through. So, he had decided to test them and see if he could travel for a while in the safe knowledge his hard earned 'retirement fund' was increasing and would do so into the future. He had set them a task to raise £20k without his involvement. He knew there was no legit way to generate cash like that in a short space of time, so they would have to take some risks, probably deal with a few people who could give them a fright if they pushed their luck too far and that was ok, because he was around if his name was needed. He had to know if they were ready to start taking over the business and, in his mind, this was an easy test to help him know one way or the other.

Together they had all it takes to be a formidable partnership as Dean was brave, tough and liked the thought of being a 'name' so people showed him respect. He could get whatever he wanted without loads of grief, due to his aggressive front and reputation. Rich on the other hand had been given the looks and the brains, but he could be a bit too sensitive for his own good at times. It was a dog eat dog world they lived in and thankfully Dean was ferocious enough for them both. Rich would think of ways to make money and Dean would make sure they got paid. Yeah, he slumped back in his leather office chair and beamed; if the lads came through, the easy life was on the cards before too much longer.

The salesman had said this chair was the choice of professionals, executives if you like, and that had pushed Russ's buttons as that was the image he liked people to see; local boy done good, entrepreneur or businessman. Anything of that nature was music to the ears and he would parade his wealth openly to embed that picture in people's heads. So what if his swivelling, dipping, deep leather chair had cost a few thousand, he had earned the money and with that the right to spend it however he chose.

It had also cost him a few thou to silence that stupid solicitor, who had poured scorn on his right to call himself a businessman at some swish party they'd been at. The beating he delivered had been worth each and every penny it had cost him.

Knob!

What a funny world; it cost roughly the same for a fancy chair as it did to put that arrogant bastard in hospital for a few nights. Based on the crack of teeth as my foot came into contact with that big mouth, perhaps I should be a jolly good fellow and send him my dentist's number. Yeah, right. Fuck him, he was lucky to get off as lightly as he did.

CHAPTER 4.

"Never underestimate a man who overestimates himself." - Franklin D. Roosevelt.

Rav was not happy as he made his way to Donna's flat. He had worked really hard to get his accountancy and business qualifications and here he was, yet again, being a messenger. Why could they not send some thick heavy to do this? He was the bookkeeper, the accountant or whatever title was bestowed on people who carried out a job role like his. He was charged with avoidance of paying tax, maximising revenue through investments, kosher or not, and laundering of monies for a fee. Surely that level of responsibility should afford him more respect than this? He made Russ a shit load of money and still he was treated as a gofer.

The person he had been sent to see lived in a shitty part of town and his designer gear was so out of place he felt like he had a big sign over his head pointing at him. If he had known he was to venture to this 'slum', he would have worn some old jeans or something more appropriate, but here he was in a Teal, skinny-fit suit, silk tie and shoes that quite probably cost more than most people round here paid for a car.

He would stick with Russ for a while longer as the money was so good, and then see what happened when the old man decided to pass on the running of the 'empire'. Who knows, he might be able to get a bigger share of the profits then. He was in his early thirties and wanted out of work by 40. Why not? Everyone wants that, and he had chosen a path that could make it a reality. Whilst his hands were slightly soiled by the things he had seen and been involved with, he had learnt to live with it and kept his eyes on the prize of being beyond the need to work ever again at a tender age. Certainly compared to most of the morons who worked to 60 plus. However, days like this made him feel so insignificant and that was so not how he saw himself, but arguing was pointless. As always, he did what was asked and would filter a little off the top in the coming days to make them pay for treating him in such a crap way. That kept him going and he smiled in a smug, self-satisfied way as he sought out the address he had been given.

* * *

Rich to Dean, "So, do you think we should have told Rav of his very important job today, so he didn't need to garb himself up quite so much?" Dean was enjoying this, "Well of course we should have, but just think, he stands out here for his OTT dress sense so in the middle of scum central he can be in his element; majestic. In fact, the natives will probably call him majesty." They laughed out loud, but it served the prat right. Russ was a smart operator and he knew full well who, if anyone, was creaming any money for themselves, so although Rav thought he was being clever, Russ was on to him and had made sure Dean and Rich knew. To Russ it was alright for the time being as he was a good accountant and did a very good job with the books. In fact, he was so good that if he had asked, Russ would probably have paid him as much, if not more, than he was funnelling off for himself. This way though, Russ had something to use if his book-keeper got too cocky and if they fell out he would insist on the credit being repaid with interest. He was quite happy for Rav to take a bit of rope as he could pull out the slack anytime he wanted to. The boys did not like it and told their dad so in no uncertain terms, but he told them he had it under control and in the meantime if it made them feel better, Rav could be used as an office boy as and when the need arose. Ever since he had said that, it 'arose' more and more often; funny that.

Strange that people in the business of thieving, bullying and protection get so annoyed when someone does the same thing to them. It was OK for them to relieve a few unfortunates of their cash in ways not exactly above board, but do it to them and suddenly they become kings of double standards. Their ignorance of this was understandable as they'd never known anything different and, in their world, loyalty was extremely important. Important, but not expected. Seasoned men like Russ trusted no-one and far too often that mistrust was vindicated. Maybe he did have an overactive nasty streak, ruthless even, and his priorities could be questionable, but you did not climb as high as he had on any greasy pole, without having a sharp brain and good instinct.

Rav's eventual undoing would certainly not have anything to do with his intellect, it was more likely to be that he was trying to be too street clever, in a world where disciplinary action was very different to the corporate world. 'You have lost your bonus' is somewhat different to 'which bones do we break first'. He was very confident by nature and growing more complacent due to what he felt were his irreplaceable skills. For an onlooker that spelled trouble, especially in a world where violent retribution is second nature, but sometimes it is hard to see the blatantly obvious when it is you. Get cocky with hot water and you get scalded. Get cocky with Russ and you get burnt.

The job he had been given today was quite simple. Call on Donna, tell her about the plans being laid for her next fight, take the brunt of her annoyance and then explain why it was in her best interests to toe the line. Face to face was the only way to do this as it left no trail and was the only way to judge how responsive the target was going to be. Dean and Rich would give it a couple of days and then follow up on Rav's foundation laying. If she was subservient in her response, then Rav could keep talking to her and pass on their wishes. However, that was always unlikely, so once he had broken the ice and she'd had a couple of days to stew on it, then they would make contact; that usually helped the reality set in and removed any poorly considered resistance.

Still people did resist. If the mention of Russ, a visit from his sons and even a scare from Chan, the colossus of a man who was an enforcer for the family, had not guaranteed total cooperation, then it was time to get heavy. Some of the guys Russ employed, or contracted in, were evil and enjoyed dishing out an X rated calling card. Nail guns, hammers and bolt cutters were all tools of their trade and one even preferred a small blow torch. If they were called on, these items were not just used for the visual impact they might have. By then it was too late and those who had been crazy enough to stand up to Russ, were going to suffer badly. Melting skin has a whiff and tang that you will smell and taste forever.

These guys had their own little sayings, like 'Pride comes before disfigurement'. They were a last resort, but get that far and you had gone too far.

CHAPTER 5.

"When dealing with people, remember you are not dealing with creatures of logic, but with creatures bristling with prejudice and motivated by pride and vanity." - Dale Carnegie.

Here it is. Not even a bell! Rav tapped quite loudly on the door and made sure he looked as distinguished as possible, first impressions and all that, he wanted this person to know he was someone of importance. As the door opened he clocked a nice face, no makeup mind, and a body that was fit in so many ways. "You Donna?" Silence. "Are you Donna?" She had not broken her stare yet and showed no sign of opening her mouth to respond. What she knew was the only people dressed like that, who knocked on doors in this neighbourhood, were either politicians, religious fanatics or people trying to flog stuff. She did not have the time or inclination to chat to any wannabee MP or councillor, because they all seemed outright liars to her, she had never been a woman of faith and she had no spare money for whatever was being sold. She always waited for them to tell her why they were knocking and then she closed the door or said, 'Not today, thank you,' depending on how she felt from her first impression.

"Tell you what, as the question seemed to prove quite difficult for you, I will assume you are Donna and will explain the purpose of my business here today. May I come in?" Same cold stare, although he could not truly say it was emotionless as he felt there was a terrible rage going on behind those eyes. "Oooo-Kaaay," he said in a mocking, but to him quite humorous way. "We will conduct our business here on your fine doorstep. My client would like to discuss a business transaction regarding your next fight." Nothing, same steely stare. "Quite the conversationalist, aren't we? I'm not sure you understand me, so to be clear this discussion WILL be happening and you WILL be doing business with my client." He could have said boss, employer or something similar, but client made him sound more significant and he liked that. "Right, the business at hand is that you do not win your next fight and then your family remain safe." He was getting tired of the stare now and so he blurted it all out to see how she would react. "Wait there," she said as the cheap door was closed in his face. Even without the business element of their discussion, Donna had not liked the look of this prick from the moment she had opened the door. Flash clothes, too shiny shoes and a way of talking to her that said, 'know your place darling'. Fuck him.

At least he knew she was not a mute! He was growing more and more tired of this crap mission he had been sent on and now this stupid girl had shut the door on him. He was not putting up with this and he thumped hard on the door. “Hey, open this door now or things will get very bad, very quickly.” He stepped back, and it was almost as if he would begin stamping his feet and throwing things if he did not soon get his way.

The door opened wide this time and he noticed her expression was more animated, even if it was still freezing cold towards him. "Keep your voice down. Who did you say you worked for?" Aha, he thought, progress. "I did not, but it's.........." What Donna knew was that he was likely to blink or look away or in some way let his guard down in response to the question. That is when the knuckle duster, propelled by arms made to punch and trained to do so with devastating effect, would land on his smug, expensively moisturised chin. He did not see it coming and he slumped to the floor in the way you see blocks of flats collapse when they get blown up. His legs gave way and then the top half of his body simply folded onto his legs. She stood over him; "Any smart comments now?"

She went back inside and placed the duster back in the drawer and called the kids. "Maggie, go and get Layla; QUICKLY!!!" Maggie scarpered next door and Sam was grinning as he saw the man on the floor outside the front door. "Did you do that to him?" She did not have time to think how best to respond to the fact she had just laid out some bloke who had dared threaten her family. "Never mind that, go and get your shoes on." Maggie returned with Layla. "What the f.......," she caught herself as she knew Donna did not like swearing in front of the kids, no idea why as they heard it all over the estate and at school, but that was up to Donna. "His sales patter not to your liking then?"

Layla made a joke out of everything and Donna gave her a dampened grin. "Who is he?" The red mist descended again as she recalled his 'offer'. "I have no idea," Donna shrugged. "Well unless he's very tired, I'm guessing he did something that you didn't appreciate.” Donna leaned in and whispered in Layla's ear, conscious of Maggie and Sam straining to hear what was being said and equally conscious of not wanting to scare them by blurting out what this idiot had said. Layla turned and kicked him in the thigh; it was a timid kick and immediately she stepped away in case he leapt up, but in her mind, it was a show of support for her mate.

Donna and Layla had been neighbours for a couple of years and friends for the same amount of time. They both liked a giggle and were of similar ages, but mostly they just clicked and instantly looked out for the other one. Layla lived on her own and she was quite happy to babysit, as she adored Maggie and Sam. Equally, it was no bad thing that through Donna’s boxing mates, idiots thought twice before messing with her.

"What's the plan?"
"I want him away from here pronto, so we need a few quid and then we can get Jiz and his boys to ship him out. Have a look and see if he has got any money on him."

Layla checked his jacket pockets, "His wallet is there, but he only has cards, no cash." "What about the trouser pockets." Layla looked at her with disbelief. "Get on with it, since when have you been scared of a cock?" She screwed her face up and said, "I am not scared, just choosey about which ones I touch." Donna grabbed Maggie and Sam by their wrists; "Go find Jiz and tell him I have got a paying job for him, but I need him sharpish." She kept hold of them; "Be quick getting back." She knew he would soon come round and she wanted him gone when that happened.

Jiz was the leader of the local teenager crew and not the sort to get on the wrong side of, as his boys could make your life hell. He had been a pupil of PD for a couple of years, before deciding boxing was too disciplined for him. He knew Donna through that.

Layla gingerly felt in Rav's pockets and produced a money clip with several 20's folded into it. "Ohhh, bingo!" Donna grabbed it off her, removed one 20 and told her to put the rest back. "Spoilsport. Can I put it in the inside jacket pocket?" Donna looked at her as if to say, why do you need to ask me that, with all I have going on. "I do not care where you put it; anyway why?" Layla pulled her pretend sick face and said, "Commando."

The kids returned a few minutes later and let Donna know Jiz would be there in a while with a couple of his boys.

Sam wanted to do his bit to help Donna, so he was already going through his Owen Farrell homage, as he addressed the 'rugby' ball. He bent his knees, looked up at some imaginary rugby posts, then back at the ball at his feet. In his head he did the 'evil eye', as he drew the line he intended the ball to take just as he had seen his hero do. All he needed was for Rav to start coming round and then he would straighten his back, step forward and smash the ball through the posts with perfect arm movement and follow through of the kicking leg. He already had his 'Joining Jack' victory salute planned. Donna spotted him leaning forward from the hips, over the unconscious body on her doorstep.
"Sam, what are you doing?"
"If he wakes up I'll kick him in the balls."
"Do what? No need for that Sammy, you keep away from him please. Get back inside."
"But what about if he's angry?"
"Not sure how you think kicking him there will help, but you don't need to worry, it's all under control. Now, please get inside with Maggie."
Sam slouches in, not hiding his annoyance that his efforts were not appreciated.

"Sam! Thank you."
Smile, skip and one happy little boy runs in the flat.

* * *

A relative calm had returned as the kids were tucked up in bed, having had lots of stories and cuddles to stop them thinking too much, as that would mean interrupted sleep and Donna did not need that tonight. Jiz had collected the package and dumped it God knows where, but she and Layla had hidden his wad of notes before they would let them get anywhere near him. The obvious place would have been down his pants, but he did not wear any. Jiz would definitely check his pockets for cash, but delving into his underwear was another thing altogether. They decided to conceal it in his sock, taped to the bottom of his foot. Donna knew she might have been in bother just for laying him out, so if he woke up and he had been relieved of that much cash, things could get really complicated. Chances were, he would not even miss that one note, but all of the folded currency, was another thing. She told Jiz that she did not know who he was, but as he had a 'client' she would not recommend taking anything that could be traced back to them, like the expensive looking watch, for example.

"Man, cause it's you, I will take him, but I will not be relieving him of anything precious; this dude works for Russ Tomkins."
"You sure? How do you know him?"
"I make it my business to know, so I don't mess where I shouldn't be. Shit Donna, you laid out one of the Tomkins employees."
"Fuck! Well get rid of him please, here's £20."
"Thanking you. Unlike you, I will treat him gentle."

* * *

Layla was a street girl and had seen her fair share of fights and general aggro, but even now it still messed with her to a certain degree. She could feel the shaking in her hands as she washed them. With all the activity going on she had not noticed, but as soon as it stops, the mind tips the body off there was danger and the brain releases the tension as only it knows how. It made her angry that at a time when her mate needed her, here she was acting like a wimp. Her annoyance was taken out on the soap, taps and towel as all were manhandled roughly. She looked in the mirror and used both hands simultaneously to slap her face as she began to pull herself together. Another look, a quick scrunch of the hair and then she stared into her eyes as they reflected back at her. It was no use, she could stay there all night, but what good would that do for Donna? She laid her hands flat on the worktop, placing them either side of the sink and then almost involuntarily, her head dropped and eyes closed. A quick dip of the arms and then she threw the whole top half of her body upwards, opening her eyes and raising her head up as part of moving on from being this useless lump, cowering in a bathroom, to being the supportive friend her mate so needed right now. With that she flung the door open and purposefully headed to the living room.

As she sat down near her friend, Layla got relatively serious for once. "You have done some daft shit in the past, but let me see if I can recall anything coming close to laying out one of the local hard men's workforce. Nope. That's official, a new personal best. To beat this, you will need to travel to Sicily and start lumping into those bastards." Donna could try and explain, but she knew her temper had got the better of her once she thought the kids were being threatened. Normally her emotions were in control, but certain things just got to her. She melted into the settee, with her head resting on the back and her hands covering all of her face.

"He didn't say who he worked for," half whispered through her fingers.
"Did you even ask?"
"Well sort of. I asked, so he would be off his guard for when I clocked him....... worked like a dream as well."
"Not like you to cheat" Layla teased.
"How is that cheating? He is a man and I am just an average sized girl, so all I did was even the odds a little." Layla aped open mouth disbelief.
"Man, what man? Did you notice his hands? They were so well preserved I would imagine they spend most of their time in thick gloves. He has not done anything manual ever and certainly has never been in a fight, I mean your daughter would have stood half a chance." Donna emerged from behind her hands and hugged Layla.
"What am I going to do now? I have fucked up so bad this time."
"You are going to do whatever they want you to and hope all this goes away as quickly as it came. For some reason that reminds me of my first boyfriend." They released, and Donna mustered the makings of a grin.

"I do know you will not like doing it. I also know you will be bleating and grumbling about it from now until it is over and what's more, I DO NOT CARE. However, if you show any signs of not going through with it, I will kick your scrawny little arse from here to kingdom come." With that she cuffed Donna across the side of her head. Donna slowly looked up at her mate with a glare that Layla had seen many times.
"That's just a taster lady, *so do not go messing with me, or I will take you out in round three,*" it was her Muhammed Ali impression and she loved using it. Silence. Layla lets out a scream, leaps up and heads out of the door as Donna makes a lunge for

her.
"I'm only running to protect you......"

CHAPTER 6.

"He who permits himself to tell a lie once, finds it much easier to do it the second time." — Thomas Jefferson.

"Let me get this straight," Rich was trying to stay straight faced as Rav told them what had happened. Dean was having a great time and he knew Rich was not done by a long shot. "You got laid out by a girl?" Rav was pissed, really pissed. He had woken up in a wheelie bin with a massive headache. "I want her taught a lesson, I want her hurt, because she disrespected us." Rich bristled a little and said, "Who gives a shit what you want? You do not mean US? You mean, she disrespected YOU. Well from what you said a minute ago you did not even get as far as saying you were from us, because you had thrown a tantrum no doubt and did a crap job of doing something very simple."

The stern look on Rich's face gradually diminished, and he continued in his earlier vein; mocking tones wrapped up as caring, but he was not doing it very well. "This monster of a girl, was she huge, bulging biceps, was it....... Wonder Woman?" Dean lost control and he turned away laughing really loud. "Wonder Woman," he shouted out and off he went again. You bastards, Rav thought, and he began to walk out. If these wastes of space were not going to do anything, he would speak to Russ and seek some retribution from him. Either way he would be taking just a little more for himself to make these two wankers pay for this. "Rav," Dean called to him, "Sorry mate, come on you can see how funny this is. Now listen, do you mind asking Carly to bring us in a couple of coffee's please?" Rav was half buying into this when Dean continued, "Second thoughts, I will get them; if she mistakes your request for an Americano as something sexual, we could have another massacre on our hands." They collapsed into more fits of laughter and Rav stormed out with his calculator of a brain totting up the bill they would 'pay' him for this day.

Once order was restored Dean said, "As I do not think another Rav visit to be a good idea, I guess we had better deliver our business proposition ourselves." Rich wiped his eyes, "Yeah, but she does sound like a real firebrand, so let us make it as easy as possible. I know what we will do, leave it to me."

CHAPTER 7.

You learn who you really are in a fight – what you're really made of. You have to face yourself and rise above your own fears and failings. – Tami Hoag.

A knock at the door and Donna grabbed Sam by his hood as he had started to make a bee line to see who it was. He was flung back in his chair and just looked at Donna. As she never knew who would be there, she did not take any chances, so she preferred to answer it. "Keep up that stare and no TV tonight. I get the door - you know that." He did and her TV threat, plus her angry look turned his head to stare deep into his half-finished plate of food and he accepted defeat. As she opened the door she saw two similar looking blokes, but one was trying too hard to look like a professional gent, with his suit buttoned up and revealing a Windsor knot on his silk tie, over a very white shirt. The other wore a suit too, but his jacket was unbuttoned as were the top two buttons on his pale blue shirt. He did not look the sort to like ties. He came across as chilled out, whilst the other one looked really het up. What Donna did not know was that this was exactly how they liked it to be. Dean had cropped hair, loved to look smart and wanted to impress everyone he met instantly with what they saw. The result was he looked like a nightclub doorman, who had been forgetting his steroids. Rich on the other hand knew he looked good, as his luck with the ladies had confirmed over and over, and his relaxed style suited him far better than being strangled by a top button and tie. The sides of his head were cut short, with his hair longer on top and with a rummaged look as though it had been combed through and then he had ruffled it with his hands.

"You Donna?" Dean asked. Nothing. "You met a friend of ours earlier, does that help you reclaim the use of your voice?" He said this with no small amount of annoyance coming through. "Wait there," she said and closed the door. Perhaps they would like a piece of what that prick earlier had got, she thought, and headed for the knuckle duster. She closed the door where the kids were and headed for the front door again, but as she opened it the whole world was blocked by a man mountain. She looked up and took an inadvertent gasp of air. "This is Chan," she heard a voice from behind him say, "and you can swing your little fist with a horseshoe in it and he won't even feel it." Chan grinned at her and stepped back as his job was done. He was dark skinned, but with an Oriental look to his eyes and he was well over 6 feet and must have weighed 20 stone plus. He was bulky without being fat and she knew this would not be a fight she could win. She thought she heard a voice saying "Christ!"

However, she was so surprised at this human wall she had come up against, she was not sure if it was hers or not.

"You have met Chan, I'm Rich, this is my brother Dean and you must be Donna," the cool one said, "so now we've got the introductions out of the way can we come in please?" He said with a naughty boy grin on his face. She was motionless, so the other one just barged in, saying "Good." She moved aside, because he would have made heavy contact with her if not. Powerless to stop them she said, "just watch yourselves as I have got kids in there" she nodded at the closed door and then pointed to the living room. She followed them in, whilst Chan stayed near the front door.

The hard looking one spoke at her, "Before you rendered our useless prat of a colleague into a deep sleep, nice duster by the way, we believe he told you the nature of his business with you. We are here to follow up on this. His client, and our old man, is Russ Tomkins; have you heard of him?" He asked this in a nonchalant sort of way, but it was loaded with menace. Of course she had, everyone in the vicinity knew of Danger-Russ Tomkins and even though she tried not to show it, she knew the fear his name brought out in people had not been lost on these two. He grinned really horribly at her and again he just said, "Good." She knew, and he definitely knew, that she would behave herself from now on, as Russ was not a man to mess with.

The cool one took over. "The nature of our business is that we do not offer people like you, choices. So let's not waste a load of time and get him anymore steamed up. For your next fight we will set you up with a patsy, which means the odds will be heavily on you winning. Unexpectedly though, you will lose and as we will be betting heavily on the patsy, we will make a few quid. You of course can then get on with your life, your boxing and, of course, punching unsuspecting accountants who knock on your door." If she was not so angry she might have liked his humorous comment. "How the fuck do I carry on with my boxing if some waste of space wipes me out and how do I know you will leave me alone even if I do agree?"

Dean spoke, "I do not give a stuff about what happens next and you do not get any guarantees about anything from us. I might come back in a year's time and ask you to take another fall. You will do it, or I will hurt you, or someone you hold precious, or both. Are you starting to get it now, you dopey cow?" Menacing monotone was a Dean special and she had just been on the receiving end of it.

Rich noticed her hands curl into tight little balls, and that coupled with the emotion oozing out of her eyes, when Dean had mentioned hurting her family, and he could sense she was about to go for his brother. He stood up and positioned himself between them. "Whoa! Dean you have had your fun, now get outside and remember it's a girl you are putting the frighteners on," their eyes locked for a second. "Girl, man, wild animal; as you know I am not worried about anyone or anything and she needs to know I mean business." "Then your work here is well and truly done, so do as I ask and step outside; please." He raised his eyebrows high, causing his eyes to fully open and he did a tiny nod in the direction of the door, as if to say leave this to me. Dean knew what his brother meant, the persona that had taken over him was no longer necessary to make sure this silly girl would play ball. "OK, but you and me are having words later," he said whilst pointing a finger in annoyance straight at his brother's face. Rich continued to keep up the stare he was sharing with Dean, but he was also making a slight grin appear as he knew this would break the stalemate. "You brother are a right prat," said Dean, "I know," Rich countered, "we could be twins."

Once Dean had gone and the door had stopped shuddering in its frame, Rich looked at Donna and said, "Listen, life ain't fair, this ain't fair, but you will take a fall when we say or you will regret it. Suck it up, take it on the chin or whatever it is you say, but get your head right about this. You know of our dad, so you know there is no way we can back down from what we have set out to do with you. I am sure that aside from a desire to thump everyone who knocks on your door you are a nice girl. Get through this, get on with your life and we will just become a bad memory. Make this easy. Now, wha' da ya say?"

There was a slight pause as she regained her composure and then in a very assured voice she said, "I am a nice girl, but so far life has dealt a bitch of a hand to me. Scum like you, albeit daddy's little spoilt brat scum, will not beat me, because none of the other crap I have had to deal with has. Whilst I am bringing up two children on next to nothing, you are poncing about putting frighteners on single mum's like me. All to make daddy proud. I do not sleep well, because I worry about the life I am giving them, but you cannot sleep at all with the damage you do to people's lives you worthless piece of shit." Rich looked at her and thought, crikey this girl has some fire and some guts, but she had stopped him in his tracks with her comments. "I sleep just fine," he said with an air of cocky arrogance. "Then you are an even worse piece of shit than I thought."

"I am trying to help, but I am not staying for any more of this. We will be in touch and you........stay safe."

"I can hardly wait; and you........go fuck yourself."

He nodded at Chan to leave and closed the door behind him. He waited for a few seconds. Would she start to cry now he was gone? He heard her voice, "Come on you two off to bed now EVEN THOUGH WE HAVE A PERVERT OUTSIDE THE FRONT DOOR." He grinned and started to walk away and then from inside he heard a little boys voice say, "What's a pervert........?"

CHAPTER 8.

In this world all I have is my word and my balls and I do not break them for anybody. - Al Capone.

Russ was tipping his chair back, resting his elbows on the arms and pushing the tips of his fingers together. He had been actively practising this since he saw someone hard, but in a suit, doing it as he really liked the look. I am sophisticated, but do not mess with me, is what it said to him when he saw it. It was so him. "I am very much looking forward to hearing what you have put together boys, hit me with it." This was their father and yet it felt more like they were in front of a headmaster, a boss at work or someone else of authority who was not related to them. The truth was the father to son relationship in this family was emotionally unattuned. In fact, to the point they did not really know him that well beneath the surface. He was certainly a father to them, though he could get a bit heavy handed, from time to time as they were growing up. All things being equal, they knew he meant well towards them. His had been a life of long hours, late hours and when he did come in there was not any reading of books together or playing games. As they got older they realised this was because he had probably been doing a bit of business, which could mean anything from giving someone a hiding, doing a job that involved a shooter or meeting with a 'colleague' when one of them felt the other was encroaching on their patch. However, business always meant a certain amount of danger and heaps of adrenaline followed by a rush of testosterone. Playing happy families did not fit too well after nights like that. Truth be told there were many such nights every week, as he carved out his danger—Russ tag and reputation. They also knew that he had given them a good life in terms of material possessions, they did not want for much, if anything. Plus, of course, nobody messed with them as they had grown up.

"Well dad," Dean began, "we have kept it simple, as we know that's what you always say works best; haven't we Rich?" Fucker; Rich thought. He's opened up the chat like he's the main man on this and then landed the detail on me. I look like his bitch. "That's right bruv, but don't let me stop you if you want to carry on with telling dad all about it." 15 all. Dean was a rabbit caught in the headlights and his jaw hung wide open with no sounds coming out. "No? Alright then, I will fill in the gaps," nice try Dean, but now all concerned knew what had just happened. Russ certainly did. He grinned at Rich, wagged a finger at Dean in a real piss take way and then said, "If you girls have finished scratching each other, can I hear what you have cooked up;

PLEASE?"

"As Dean said it is simple, a flutter seemed to be a good option, especially if we stacked our hand. We had a chat around and as there is always plenty of cash being flashed at Boxing, that seemed worth a second look. Then we hear about a girl who could go on to be quite big in the game, as ladies fighting is really taking off. So, we have lined up this tasty bird boxer to take a fall against a right patsy and we will clean up as the odds will be rather favourable." Russ leaned back a bit more, then rolled to the side and never once did he let his fingertips part. "Dad, this is not Dragons Den; do you like it?" Rich was cocky enough to crack a line like this, but his dad was wily enough not to re-act.

He held an icy stare for some time. He knew just about every scam there was, and his mind was running through the pro's and con's and what he needed to know to be sure it would cough up. "Has anyone told her?" Without a 'willing' party he knew this was not getting off the ground, so he wanted to know what they had done to be sure of her agreement. "Rav tried," the boys shot each other a juvenile grin, "and then we delivered the message. She is all but signed up, but we will do a little more hammering of our point over the coming days to be sure. She has kids, so she will not risk anything happening to her or them." Dean was pleased to be speaking.

"You delivered the message?" Russ asked "Yep," said Dean with something of a vocal swagger. "Is that why you needed Chan the other night?" The old Fox did not miss anything. "Who is her manager, how much will we clear and which biscuit will take the pounding?" All great questions from someone who had been there, done that and nearly worn a ball hammer many times for trying. Had they done the background work or were they daft enough to think there was such a thing as easy money. Dean looked at Rich as if to say, "Well?" Rich knew the difficult questions would fall in his lap, so even though he was expecting the hand-off from Dean, he thought he would make him sweat a bit and gave him a WTF look.

Then he turned to his dad. "It's PD. Once he heard we were from the Tomkins clan we guessed he would be amenable. Was that your word or mine, Deano?" Middle finger salute from Dean. "We expect to easily clear £20k as we know it's not a new game in town. By keeping it low we'll get away with it without too much hassle. The bookie looks like being Stoney and that will be the biggest hurdle. However, we will set up a few corporate days from your people to give him an in to a few nice pay days, so if it does go tits up he will have banked a few quid and shouldn't make much of a fuss. If that does not work Dean will have been getting friendly with his missus and she will take the heat off us. Nothing is certain dad, you know that, but we have thought it through. We are out to show you we can start to take on more of the business. Dean, anything to add?" Double middle finger salute.

Russ kept leaning back, rolling from side to side and pressing those finger tips. "It's not bad, not bad at all. PD was good thinking as he's not daft enough to take me on, but he is a tough old bastard so no getting too cocky as he might shock you yet. Plus, I love the old sod, no-one touches him without my nod; get it?" Both dipped their heads in agreement. "I am sure most of that was your work.........Dean." Rich knew the old man liked the plan as he was cracking jokes. Men like Russ, hard men, or corporate executives all too pleased with their status, are seldom naturally funny, but no-one ever tells them they're not. When they crack rubbish lines like this, everyone waits for their lead and then joins in. Russ grinned and then erupted into a roar of a laugh. He was not at all surprised to see the room falling about. Dean was not about to give the middle finger to his dad, so he put one finger to his nose and pointed at his dad with the fingers of the other hand and said, "You know it." It was a good response and yet they all waited to see if Russ liked it before committing themselves. He did and promptly did the same back to Dean, before turning it into a middle finger salute and again waited for the room to erupt at his comic genius.

Russ continued, "£20k is small feed, but sensible. As for Stoney, I like the A, B and C plans and it is just lucky that we have a member of the family who does not care where he dips it for the benefit of the business. Dean you get on that quickly in case we need his missus on board. Get on that.........how funny am I?" He did not look around as he was deep into his thinking. "The fact is Stoney has survived in a tough business, because he is hard, smart and makes a point of paying back with interest, so we will tread carefully. I want to meet this 'tasty' bird we are investing our money in." Rich had not expected that and certainly Dean hadn't. They were not sure why, but for some reason this unnerved them, and Russ sensed it.

"Problem?" He half smirked as he said it as he liked wrong footing people, even his own sons. "Of course not. It's just you wanted us to prove we could look after a bit of business ourselves and this does not feel much like that." Rich was mega impressed with his brother's intervention, go Dean. "Ah, there there. Daddy hurt your feelings, has he? Now man up. When is a good time?" Dean again, "I will set it up for........" Russ interrupted, "Tomorrow." For the first time his fingertips parted as he clasped his hands behind his neck. "I am looking forward to it and I hope she is a knockout." He grinned at his feeble joke, but this time the normal torrent of laughing was met by silence.

Rich and Dean felt a bit deflated. It was like he was taking over and it pissed them off enough to make their feelings known, by not laughing at his joke. Russ saw these would be gangsters acting like petulant little boys, but it was no surprise to him. His fault, as he had spoiled them. They had led a privileged life, but whilst he was prepared to give them some rope the fact that they were still using his reputation as part of the plan did concern him. However, if that was how they wanted it he would need to know a bit more of what was planned and who was involved. Business, then family; a simple creed that had given him riches aplenty and whilst not exactly providing a stable family life, he would stick with what had worked out pretty well for him so far.

CHAPTER 9.

"Nothing personal, it's just business." – Otto Berman.

PD was deep in thought and not a little worried about what Donna was telling him in his tiny office, when there was what can only be described as a silent commotion in the gym. Chan was used to the effect he had when he entered a room. He had perfected it over many years to the point where he could prevent trouble just by the way his arrival seemed to coincide with all the oxygen leaving. He emerged through the door and just stood, looking slowly all around the room, catching as many eyes as he could and soaking up the fear he was creating. He did not make any attempt to stare anyone out, he just clocked those who looked down, those who didn't, but were not worth wasting any effort on, and those he could see from their eyes wanted to have a go and given any encouragement might foolishly do so. Once he had the room's attention, he made way for Russ and any hangers on with him. As they made their entrance, he scanned again and sought out those eyes he felt needed a bit more intensity, second time round. He assessed how tough they were acting once his bulk was side by side with one of the hardest known members of this or probably any community.

Russ entered as he always did, gazing down at his feet, rocking back on his heels and then slowly lifting his head to make sure everyone was looking at him. If anyone was not, he stared until they did and then gave them a wink as if to say, 'I'm the daddy' At this point Chan knew if it was ok or at what state of readiness he needed to be.

Russ had not been to PD's gym for quite a while, as his boxing tuition days were well behind him. He could not believe how little had changed. He loved the feel of this place; his nostrils filled with all those basic smells that cannot be avoided in a fighting environment, along with the whiff of leather and ointments. The speed ball coming to a halt was about the last sound to die out and the quiet was, in his eyes, a victory already. Chan registered the mood and loosened up a little.

The silence was broken by PD emerging from his office at a speed not usually associated with him. He headed for the guests. "Russ, good to see you...careful you do not get some sweat on your suit." He knew that humour could crack the silence and it did as he caused a few grins, but Russ wanted total control of the room. He came back with, "Never mind about sweat, if any blood gets on it I can guarantee it will not be mine." He locked eyes with PD for a few seconds and then began to walk towards the office. "Hey Chan," blared PD, "you've put on a few pounds," as he playfully punched his gut, "like 40!!!" Chan really liked PD and put a huge arm round his shoulder as they followed Russ, "I am doing OK old man, good to see ya. Some of your boys look ready to have a go; make sure they don't." There was no threat in his voice, just common sense advice, so PD turned to everyone and said, "It's OK, just carry on as you were. Wayne, that heavy bag just phoned me to ask if you will stop tickling it......" Mocking fingers pointed at Wayne, one finger replied. Then he ran as one of the heavyweights headed his way after this show of disrespect.

Donna knew who had arrived, and why. The red mist was descending. However, despite the overwhelming frenzy her temper was inflicting inside her head, she had decided on a way to deal with this situation. It meant even though she would not be in control of it, she would maintain some control over it. As Russ and his crew filled the tiny space, thank heavens Chan stayed outside, she locked her eyes on Rich and did not break from her eyeballing. Russ immediately engaged with her, "So I understand you are going to make me some money." She did not look or acknowledge him at all, instead she kept looking at Rich and said, "If you," she pointed at Rich, "or any of this lot, touch that silly old bastard out there, or any of my family, I will become a problem that even hiding behind daddy will not be able to prevent." The stare was icy, solid and sincere. PD squeezed his way in and found Donna in a stare off with Rich. Dean had his mouth open again, not knowing what to do, and Russ getting very red in the face; a sure sign that his well renowned temper was erupting. "What the fuck happened in here" PD said.

Russ was shocked at the gob and cheek of this girl. If she was not about to earn me a few quid, this little slut would not have a throat left. Reputationally, he was beyond proving a point of how ruthless he could be when provoked, but even so, he was not going to just let it lie. "Do you have any idea who the fuck you just ignored in order to launch an attack on my son, that quite frankly I can't see you being able to carry out? This is business and you have got yourself mixed up in it little lady. Now, let me be very clear on this; if you ever insult me again or even begin to threaten me or mine, then I will show you that I do not make empty promises and one of your two kids or your friend next door will regret it."

She blinked as his threat was processed in her brain, but continued to target her eyes purely on Rich. Donna and the boys both wondered how he had known about the personal stuff, but of course he had not got to the position he held in his profession, without doing some homework. "Now you look at me, before I forget what a gentleman I am." The stare started to thaw and she gave Rich a look that clearly told him she thought he was a pussy, a weak pussy. Then she turned to Russ. "Yes, I do know who you are. I can assure you I can fulfil my promises. This is not my business, it's yours and I did not get mixed up in it. These two......precious little darlings of yours, decided I should be a part of it. I will never insult you or even say a bad word to the Chuckle brothers again, because I am not sure what exactly that would achieve." Silence. More silence.

At this point she began to realise who she was actually talking to and as the blur cleared she could see the terror this man had caused so many people, just by looking into his horrible eyes. The scars evidenced they had been in a few scrapes, but beyond that, they were lifeless, except for the anger they let the world see. Now she was scared and wondered why she had let her massive gob put her loved ones in any danger. She was just about to start apologising, begging if necessary, when Russ filled the void.

"Good choice lads. This is one piece of work. Rich have you shit yourself yet, you big Jessie? PD, my boys have set up some business with this girl and she will see it through; you make sure of that. You are an old friend, but that does not count for much with me when business comes calling, as I am sure you know. She will do what she is told or suffer the consequences." His glare was making the point very forcefully.

All of a sudden, the intensity appeared to slowly fade and his stance noticeably relaxed. "However, after that I would like to sit down with you and discuss how good she can be and whether it is worth my while stumping up a few quid to back her." Donna remained calm. Dean and Rich dare not look at each other for fear of giggling and PD felt his jaw sag to his knees. All were thinking exactly the same; is he for real? Too many yes men over too many years had meant he was a man lacking in any self-awareness.

Donna was incredulous. She had started to believe that perhaps if she went through with this whole situation she could then get back to normal, but now Russ was considering remaining in her life as, of all things, a backer. The money would be welcome, his influence would open doors, but for fucks sake; let him get involved and she lost any control of her life. Inside she was saying go fuck yourself, but outside she was giving nothing away.

"Any of your boys got what it takes?" Russ clearly felt he had achieved what he needed to with Donna and was moving on to have a nice little chat with PD, "....and who makes the brew around here? Her?" He pointed at Donna. "Make your own brew you lazy, cocky, sexist, arsehole," was a sentence forming in her head when PD jumped in. "Nooooo. Donna has a fight coming up and needs to be in top form for it, plus when it comes to training, she's the hardest worker I have. Round here, the lazy sods do the tea making."

Russ could see PD was protective, but he was not finished demeaning her yet. "Fight? Oh yeah, fight," he winked at PD, "Run along then and let the adults speak, as I need to brief your manager here on this 'fight' of yours. 2 sugars in mine." He roared with laughter at his little quip, with of course no-one knowing if he was serious or not, so mouths half curled into pretend grins until PD did as normal and calmed things down. "As I have been the laziest and naughtiest today, I will make a drink....," and before Russ even had a chance to challenge this, PD had steered Donna out of the room saying, "Keep working on those drills from earlier..." She had no idea what he was on about, but he had maneuvered her out of a tricky situation. If I had made him a drink he would have been tasting my piss, she thought to herself and grinned at the image. "Nicely done," Russ said as PD came back in and gave him a sarcastic look that told the room he had clocked what had just happened. "You fancy her or something?" PD did not take the bait as it was intended. "Of course, who wouldn't. Now what does everyone want to drink."

CHAPTER 10.

"There are 3 ingredients in the good life: learning, earning and yearning." - Christopher Morley.

Rich sat in his car and waited. He stopped at a convenient place between PDs gym and where Donna lived. Finding out when she would be in the gym was not difficult as he stuffed twenty quid in one of the younger boy's pocket to give him the nod. Why was he doing this? Bloody girl had got right under his skin with that stupid staring thing a few days ago and Dean had not helped; he walked in to find both him and Chan wearing those fake glasses with misaligned eyes saying, "Do I scare you, big boy?" He had chased his brother, but one huge shovel of a hand from Chan left him treading air.

Something was telling him to meet her, to find out more about her and why she had targeted him. She had made him look pissy in front of both his dad and Dean, and in this family that was a major crime. He was going to have it out with her. However, he also realised that he had gone to quite a lot of bother to look good for this 'meeting'. Yeah, she was a looker, but without too much effort he was very presentable or else how come he did not have any trouble pulling good looking women. So why? "Fuck!" he said out loud unintentionally, she had done a real number on him. He tilted the rear view mirror to make sure the Ray Ban 'Clubmaster' sunglasses, were giving the look he was going for and pleased with what he saw, he put it back in position and waited again.

Here she was, he felt nervous, excited, butterflies; butterflies! In his head he was shouting 'get a grip man', but on the outside his calm demeanour was holding in an awful lot of emotion.

"Hey," he shouted as he stepped out of the black Beamer trying very hard to be mega impressive. "I want a word with you."
He had got her attention. She had been miles away, thinking about nothing in particular and now here was Mr. Up Himself to have another go.
"Well, I have got two for you; sex and travel."
"Hilarious. 'Fuck off', heard it so many times before," he faked a laugh and held his tummy to emphasise the point.
"I know what it is you're after, you want me to pay for having your trousers cleaned

after I made you piss yourself the other day." Her face was red from her work out and the adrenaline was still tearing round her body, so the quips were coming fast and true. She carried on walking at exactly the same pace and strode straight by him, avoiding the macho shoulder to shoulder hit as she deftly moved beyond him. She had no need to prove anything to him.

"Is daddy waiting in the car in case I prove too much for his little baby boy?"
"What the fuck is wrong with you?" Shit; she had done it again and got a reaction. His head slumped onto his chest and he placed his hands on his sides as he fought his annoyance. He had to control himself better, but she somehow knew how to push his buttons.

"Seriously! You want me to explain how you, and your bunch of fuckwits, have threatened me, my family and my career and then carry on like we are all old friends? I have got one for you. Based on that last useless question of yours; what the fuck is wrong with YOU?" If this was the opening round he was already reeling on the ropes.

"Yeah, it was dozy of me to ask that, jeez. But you are so difficult to talk to and I would like to know why you felt I was the one to lock on to the other day?" He had hoped to engage in a bit more chat before landing that on her, but there it was, he had told her and now it was up to her. Despite having come from the gym and recovering from the effects of a hard work out, he was impressed at how good she still looked. Some of the mingers who tried it on with him when he was out did not look this good for a night on the town. Decent trainers, cheap sweat pants, hoodie and her brown hair in that pony tail she seemed to favour. No lippy, but a hint of eye makeup and obviously she did not carry any fat. Tasty in the ring and tasty out of it, he thought, and then a curl in his lip that was about to form a grin was halted.

"Something funny in all this for you?" she delivered monotone, with no attempt to hide her disapproval. He was momentarily flustered, but soon got his composure back.

"Yeah, you! We both know I could snap you in a second and not break a sweat, so what's with all this hard front; you are a girl? Ok, so you are trying to make a name for yourself in a man's world, but who cares about women boxing? Cut the crap and answer me, before I lose my patience......."
"...... And do what, hit a GIRL?" She emphasised the word girl to make him see what a prat he was being.
"You can't snap anything without daddy's say so and of course his hired muscle, so YOU cut the crap. I can look after myself, ask your gofer when he wakes up. As for boxing, I never said I liked it and you MEN can shove it once I have got what I need from it, but I happen to be good at it and that will make a better life for me and mine. If no-one cares, then why are you getting involved in it? I am tougher than

you, smarter than you and making my own way in life, which makes me the complete opposite of you. Until you and your useless lump of a brother came along I was on my way to sorting things, but now I have got to deal with you shits and then see if I can pick up the threads or if I need to make different plans. If you do not mind, I will be on my way now and you can go and play at being a tosser somewhere else."

"Nice chatting to you," he called after her. "I will be in touch and....... I just love that arse." Let's see if a 'lad' comment will get a reaction. Donna stopped in her stride for a second or two, but then moved on without bothering to reply. It was a while before she could turn the corner and whether or not he was staring at her bum, she had no intention of giving him the satisfaction of having the last word. If he is still gawping, let me give him something to look at. She began walking in an exaggerated way really pushing her bum from side to side. Just as she turned the corner she very discreetly checked if he was still there. Then she shouted, "At least you are looking at this one rather than having your head stuck up it - like daddy dears." She turned the corner before he could say or do anything and smiled as wide as she had for a very long time; that felt good. Back at the Beamer, Rich was grinning too.

Not taking much notice of what was in front of her, she just avoided walking straight into Nahmee and through a very late shimmy managed to merely brush past him. Nahmee was one of those guys who wanted to be known as a man to be reckoned with, but who did not have the balls or the know how or in fact anything of substance to be a serious player. The police knew of him, but all for petty stuff. Like most people they treated him as an annoyance and felt their time was better spent going after bigger fish. Those bigger fish threw him a morsel every so often, that did give him enough street cred to gain a certain amount of respect in the drinking establishments he frequented, but as he could not be trusted to squeal if the squeeze was put on him, it was very low level stuff and anyone in the know was aware of his minor foot soldier status. However, if you listened to him, he would assure you he was in with all the 'Mr. Bigs' around, had been involved in some serious action and you were safe in his company.

Because of this he always seemed to have an 'apprentice' with him; young, impressionable, male and starry eyed for a life that did not involve 9 to 5 working for some little Hitler type. Much more attractive was mixing with hard guys, a bit of thieving, cash to flash, girls, cars and having a name as 'someone'; easy life. Of course, the thought of getting caught never came into their thinking, like everyone else they were clearly too smart to have the local plod nab them. The prospect of doing time for this life was not given any consideration, nor was the thought of the danger of mixing daily with men who liked to hurt people. If they looked at these thugs wrong or upset them in any way, a slap was the minimum they could expect. For people with limited career options, any selection is pretty crap, so through choice, or circumstance, they make their pick and take their chances.

Nahmee was so called because at school he had been into lipping the teachers, nicking stuff, playing hooky, and all that, and yet whenever he was in for a telling off he said, 'Nah me man'. That was until the evidence against him was too much and then he would cave, taking everyone else down with him.

Wanting to look cool in front of his current apprentice, Nahmee looked at Donna and saw she was tidy in all respects, "Anytime lady, no appointment required for you." Donna had already stopped smiling. The rapid change of emotion from self-satisfaction to this prat trying it on, was putting her brain in a spin. She blurted out, "Fuck off, you piece of shit." OK he was, but all he had done is made a cocky remark to look good in front of his side kick. No sooner had she said it than she thought, why did you not just smile and walk on? She was just about to do that, when Nahmee felt some face saving was required. "You ran into me bitch and you are not all you seem to think you are. Right now, you made a bad decision by fucking me off with that big gob of yours. You any idea who the fuck I am?"

Donna thought, do I deck him, do I run, apologise? With what had happened with Rich, how pleased she had been with herself and then this, her mind was going too fast to weigh up what to do for the best. Then the decision was taken away from her. "She does not care who you are," Rich had appeared, "neither do I. So, before you get into something you really do not want to, I suggest you and your boyfriend be on your way?"

Nahmee looked at Rich and saw he was cool and collected and had an air about him, but he did not look like a hard case. Then he looked at Donna and he could not work out if she was happy this idiot had turned up or even more annoyed by his interference. He had no intention of swinging any punches, as that was not his style at all, but to simply walk away would make him a laughing stock.
"Give me one good reason why I should," he crossed his arms and gave Rich his best stare.
"Have you heard of Danger-Russ?" Rich stared straight back.
"Of course man; you his arse wiper or something?"
"Nope, he's my old fella." Silence. "Tell you what, give me your name and I will see if he's heard of you?" Rich got out his mobile and looked at Nahmee, whilst pretending to be ready to make the call.
"Man, if you are who you say you are then this ends here, but if you are playing with me I will pay you a visit and it won't be pretty."
Rich grinned, "You are pissing me off now, so instead I will ask Chan to call on you to confirm who I am.........you can bet your life, that won't be pretty." The thought of a raging bear calling round was enough for Nahmee; everyone knew Chan.
"OK man, you just drew the winning hand." With that Nahmee was gone at half gallop. Once his mate realised what had happened, he held both hands up as if to say, 'do not shoot me' and then legged it.

"I thought he was going to piss himself," grinned Rich.
"Who the fuck do you think you are to get involved in my shit?" Donna was in his face and as he had already seen with her temper, who knows what might happen next. He slowly and carefully put his hands on the tops of her arms and stepped back before letting go. Safely out of her reach he said,
"My pleasure, no thanks needed." He produced a forced half smile.
"Thanks? You have done more to effect my life than that weed ever will and because you stopped me putting him to sleep for a while, you want thanks?" She paused. He could see she was gathering her thoughts and he braced himself for the big finale. "By the way, if you do ever want to interfere in my business again, at least do it yourself. It is up to you if you use your dad's name to fight your battles, but NEVER EVER use it to fight mine." Her voice had gradually built in volume, and feeling, to the point where she shouted part of it towards the end. The intensity of what she had said was still firing out of those eyes.

Yes, she was scary and perhaps a little crazy, but he looked at her and he knew he was feeling something inside that could only mean trouble. He also knew there was no fighting it. Those eyes were gorgeous and so was she. All of her. He so knew this was not the time to tell her! He also knew he wanted to get to know her better and although that did not make any sense, there was no disputing what was stirring inside him.

Angry, extremely angry, or not he found this girl something else. He took his time to reply as he wanted to get this bit right. He looked at his feet and shuffled a bit. Then he took his hands out of his pockets and crossed them in front of his chest, almost as if to protect himself. He looked at Donna and in a very monotone, void of emotion voice he said, "You are right. Sorry." It just hung there, between them, for what seemed like ages. Then he saw her features soften slightly and the inferno was subsiding. Perhaps he could try an incursion into enemy territory.

"Listen, that idiot might have run off, but chances are he is not too far away. If he sees me drive off, he might give you some more grief." He could see the heckles rising again as it was clear she had taken that to mean she needed protecting. He was losing control of this situation.
"and.... if he did that I could not live with myself if I let you beat the crap out of him and got into unnecessary trouble." His palms were chest high, open and facing towards her, which appeared submissive. On his face was emerging that cheeky grin.
"So even though it's a bit ridiculous in the circumstances, can I give you a lift home?"
"I hate you."
"I know. So, is that a yes?"

CHAPTER 11.

"Sometimes," said Pooh, "the smallest things take up the most room in your heart."
– A A Milne.

What on earth had possessed her to get into his car? Was it really that she worried in case Nahmee came back? She was just about to demand he pull over and let her out, the image of which was projected in high definition in her mind as she saw herself slam the car door so hard it made him jump a little in his seat, when she heard him talking.

"This might not mean much, but I do wish we had not interfered in your life......."
"But you have, haven't you? So no, it doesn't mean shit to me." She had let him have it straight and true, Donna style.
"Listen, I am trying here, give me some slack."
"Go fuck yourself."

Silence. Both staring straight ahead, Rich, not sure what he could say without getting yelled at and Donna waiting for him to say anything, so she could yell at him.

He pulled over. "You win," he stated. "I know I caused all of this and I am an arrogant bastard as far as you are concerned, but I want to see what I can do to get out of this crap situation we are in. I have absolutely no idea what that looks like I should add, but please understand just shouting at me is not going to change anything or help in any way. I will see you around no doubt."

He reached into the back to grab her hold-all when his tee shirt rose just enough for her to see his stomach. His flat, tanned stomach. Did he do that on purpose, she thought? Whatever, he had shaken her thinking and all of a sudden, she saw beyond the twat and realised he was bloody good looking and based on the small piece of flesh he had exposed, he had a good body too. As her eyes moved up, she saw that he had realised what she was looking at and he grinned. However, this was not a cocky boy grin, this was a 'I like you' grin and she returned it. Then it hit her what she was doing and in a very awkward OTT way she stopped smiling, she grabbed her bag and began fiddling with the door to get out. "How the fuck do you get out of this massive cock on wheels of a car?" He reached over and effortlessly the door was open. Seriously, she said to herself for looking even remotely silly at not being able to undo a car door. He smelt really good too!

Then she was out, bag thrown onto the pavement and door slamming just as she had seen in her mind. Except he did not jump, his eyes remained fixed on hers. Why was she not moving? She could, obviously she could, but she was not. They stared for a while and then he said, "Nice slam."

The fuss getting out of the car, her ever ready temper and chucking the hold-all about had made her breathe heavily, so she just stood on the pavement and collected herself. She became conscious of her inhaling and exhaling slowing, regulating to a more normal level. The mist was lifting, and she was seeing Rich in a very different way.

She saw his mouth move, "How about I drive you a bit further and if I say anything that winds you up, or perhaps if I say anything at all, then we stop and you can have a repeat slam? I am sure you could buckle that whole side if you practice enough." Was she softening to him at all he wondered, but not enough to follow up his quip with even a twitch of anything resembling a smile.

She eventually leant on the car. "You are sorry, but so what? Let's be realistic here, the situation we find ourselves in means we have a chasm between us. You might be a pretty boy, who in another time and place could mean something to me, but come on. Now? In all this shit? You choose to fuck with my family, my career and my one real chance of providing something at least a little bit special for two small people who have had a shit time of it in their young lives already. Not the ideal beginning to any sort of friendship wouldn't you say? Anyhow, I'm just another conquest for your inflated ego to shag. That, I do not need. You, I do not need"

"You have begun to make me see what a spoilt brat I am, and I have no business messing in other people's lives. YOU have done that. I have got you into something I shouldn't have, and I have no idea how to get out of this, but I want to try. I am not asking you to forgive me; I know you can't. I get that you do not need me and I know I am asking a lot, but I would like to get to know you. Really get to know you. Get in now and let's see what happens, or do not get in and who knows you might wonder what if. Your move."

He saw the eyes begin to burn again, "You are so far up yourself. So I have to get in now, do I? I have to decide now, whether to even begin thinking of seeing what might happen do I? Well you listen to me you deluded, obnoxious prat......" Mid her sentence he drove off and, 50 meters down the road, he stopped. Then he looked back at her. He reached over and the passenger door opened. He got out of the car and shouted to her, "Please. Get in the car and let's have another go. I've missed you." It was sarcastic, but also funny.

Time stood still. Then she picked up her bag, ever so slowly sauntered towards the car and got in with her bag on her lap, clutched to her chest. "Fucking twat," she said without taking her eyes off the road ahead. "Don't you mean, pretty boy fucking twat?" As she was about to throw a slap his way he sped off thrusting her back in her seat.

CHAPTER 12.

"Feeling lost, crazy and desperate belongs to a good life as much as optimism, certainty and reason." - Alain de Botton.

Donna laid her hand over her eyes as she thumped the back of her head into the crisp, white pillow. What have you done this time, she asked herself behind the protection of her hand. Of all the crazy, stupid, ridiculous things she had ever done this had to be top of the charts. No matter how she thought it through, she could not explain it. Rich stirred beside her. What had landed her here, with him? Was it the good looks, the charm or some prehistoric, inbuilt survival button that was pressed at the thought that he might actually be able to help. She definitely went for the last option as the first two would mean she was weak and a pathetic woman.

She had grudgingly accepted the lift, quite why she was still beating herself up for. As the chat had developed he suggested coffee to apologise for using his dad's name to help defend her and unbelievably, she had accepted. He was funny, so funny, and after a slow start the conversation had been relatively easy. He oozed a certain confidence and time flew by. He genuinely did seem to be wanting to seek a solution for this situation, but both knew it was already a runaway train. The next thing she knew here they were. She accepted the chances were she was kidding herself, but even so it was easier to believe that all this was about protecting her and the kids. If using her looks and body delivered that, then it was worth the price. Still a little voice was chirping in her ear saying, you had a good time though, you did not exactly play hard to get, and all manner of confusing messages were flooding her brain. She wanted to scream to make them stop. Any sane person could see this was about as stupid as it gets.

"Hey," he said, as he stroked her arm, "exactly, how did this happen?"
"Shall we start with the bit where you set out to make my life a misery..........." her annoyance at herself, was easier to deal with when directed at him.
"Let's not do all that again p-lease. Our worlds are different and whilst I am not asking you to like it, I am asking you to understand me in it. All things considered it is a bit weird, but I really like you and as you are laying in bed naked with me, I'm guessing you feel something similar. Trading insults is not going to get us anywhere. OK?" Now that was annoying, she had let him get the high ground and to really twist the knife, he was right. She had to admit he was her type; funny, looked after

himself physically and not bad looking at all.
"So, what do you suggest we do next then - should I get your dad on the phone?" He did not say anything, he just looked at her with both eyebrows raised and his lips stretched wide without any sign of teeth. She knew she had done it again.
"Alright, alright." Pause. "Sorry." He began to feign a heart attack as part of making the most of her having to apologise. A thump to his arm soon brought that to a halt.
"Ouch. If that was playful feel free never to get ratty with me," he winced a bit, but maintained his air of coolness; just.
"It was a baby hit, you big girl. If you do not act the idiot, it won't happen."

"Before your unprovoked attack on my persons, we were discussing what we do from here, I believe. First of all, we had better see how we both feel about things." She looked at him in a real put down kind of way.
"Things. Things!." He pulled himself up and rested his elbows on his knees and his head in his hands.
"Us. Happy now that you have made me say it? US." The mini victories were not feeling as nice to Donna and she rested her hand on his back and began stroking up and down.
"Rich, in ways you have most to lose, because if your dad finds out about us before the fight, he will not be your number one fan. I'm coming with the baggage of two kids who are not mine, but who I will always love as if they were. I have a rented flat, no money to speak of and a potential career as a boxer that either someone like you, some tough cow or any number of things could fuck up in a second. Plus, I have no intention of becoming a moll," she put her hands in the air and bent her index fingers to accentuate the word.
"Where does that leave you?" He pulled his head out of his hands and then kissed her on the shoulder,
"With a lot to gain," he said. Then they melted into each other as they laid back on the bed.
"It's beyond crazy, this whole situation, but I want you. I want to be with you and I guess everything else will have to work itself out." She liked hearing him say it and she squeezed him tight. Was it genuine or the words of someone thinking more with his dick than his head? However, she liked the thought of being with him as well, very much.

She released her grip and headed for the bathroom, "Of course, we do have a major stumbling block that you have not considered yet." She turned to see the cogs whirring in his brain. A worried, confused look emerged on his face and was joined by a frown on his brow. "Your dad fancies me rotten."

"Yeah, he has always had a soft spot for crazy girls who shout a lot and hit randomly. Then there's your big arse...." Within seconds she was on top and pummelling away playfully at him. She stopped and he emerged from behind his protective shield of a pillow. His hands cupped her face and he drew her to him.

Their mouths locked. First gently and slowly, then rhythmically, becoming more passionate and less in time with each other. Heads moving from side to side, teeth hitting every so often, but neither noticed as their tongues searched each other's mouth, seeking nothing more than pleasure.

Suddenly, Rich took charge as he swapped positions, so he was over her. His body pressing, grinding into hers, whilst he held most of his weight on his arms. He kissed where her neck met her shoulder and she writhed with the shock of the delicious electricity it caused. He continued to half bite, half suck all over her neck as her hands felt all over his back. Kneading, stroking, pulling, she was unconsciously exploring what was available to her. He moved slightly so he could carry on his journey down her arms and he sucked hard on the inside of her arm, in the well between the forearm and upper arm, and proceeded to gently bite into her elbow bone.

He felt her grabbing for his manhood, in perhaps an instinctive way for him to get a move on to her more obvious places. The half groan sound he made let them both know his rapture at the firm, ebb and flow of her pulling, thrusting grip, up and down the full length of his prick.

He knew her pleasure lay in the slow, teasing exploration of her form in places away from her obvious love zones. He knew exactly what he was doing, touching where her nerve endings would arouse her whole body as her desire and sexuality heightened. He knew where they were and he would carry on his search for them, using fingers and lips. The wait would be worth it. Then when he was ready, and she could stand it no more, he would become more frenzied, more animalistic, as their hot togetherness, developed.

She was stroking, grabbing and releasing his hair, as his lips made contact with her abdomen. He traced his way down one thigh, his tongue licked all the way down her calf bone. She felt him sucking on her toe, biting her ankle and then lips traced up the other leg; kissing, brushing as they went. She could feel his breath on her fanny. Donna screamed at the thrill it generated. He did not pause for any length of time as he began moving towards her breasts. Her breathing, those accidental sighs and her ever increasing grasping at him, disclosed the many, pleasing, sensual eruptions sparking all over her body. He locked his mouth on hers and she held the back of his head as their tongues searched each other out. At the same time, he began squeezing her breasts and caressing her nipples.

He pulled away for an instant and they looked very deep into each other's eyes for the briefest of moments, before once again their instincts took over and they merged into one, writhing form.

CHAPTER 13.

"To a father growing old, nothing is dearer than a daughter." – Euripides.

Donna did not get on with her parents. Her mum had been completely against her taking on the kids and said so, over and over. In Donna's opinion, out of pure spite she had not done anything to help them since. Not anything meaningful anyway; birthday and Christmas cards and treats, but even then, small feed. Her dad was a wrong 'un. Done time, cheated on her mum several times and was vicious if you got into a scrap with him. Winning was not enough as he liked to hurt people and he had often carried on long after the other guy had given up. It had earned him a reputation that he cashed in on regularly and even known 'faces' thought twice about mixing with him.

However, after this last stretch he had made a few quid on second hand cars and invested it wisely in property at just the right time. The result was he was now doing pretty well for himself. She had not seen him for ages and neither him nor her, had tried desperately hard to make contact, so things just trundled along without each other. He had some prissy little girlfriend, not much older than Helen would have been now, who he doted on and this girl knew her body and looks would keep him in check. Donna had the kids and her boxing and so they had little need for each other's company. Now, however, things had changed for her and she wanted to be sure the kids would be safe, no matter what happened to her. As she was not exactly flushed with options, she felt he might be worth having back in her life for the time being. Russ would know of him, as everyone knew him as Dog, which he got named after one of his ferocious, wanton attacks, on a defeated street fight opponent, and that could well make him think again about his little plan involving her.

Rich was a new problem, but the kids were always the priority and she would worry about him later. For now, she needed certainty they would be alright. A painful phone call to mum, with numerous 'I was right' comments coming at her, had given her an address and a mobile number. Even though her parents had gone their separate ways ages ago, they kept in touch for some strange reason. Donna had called and set up a catch up chat with him in a bar and was headed there now. Why the fuck am I nervous, she was asking herself in her head. This is silly, get a grip woman, he is your dad!

As Donna entered the bar she scanned the room, there he was on a table on his own with a golden pint he had taken a mouthful from. His hair was tidy and greying and quite obviously this was not a young man, but his physique and demeanour told anyone with half a brain that he was one to be wary of. His leather biker jacket, over a dark V neck tee shirt, suited him well and neither looked cheap. His jeans were modern in style and below them were sand coloured boots of the kind that imitated working men's. He has made an effort, that is for sure.

He saw her and smiled, giving away all the paternal emotions he was suffering right then. He waved to make doubly sure she had seen him and pointed at a tall clear drink next to his. So far so good, he had got her water and that had shown he was at least thinking and trying. "Hi. Thanks for the drink and for meeting me," she sat down and took a sup. "You look good my girl; fighting fit for sure. So how much pleasantries do you want to wade through before you tell me what the problem is?" She put the drink down, but continued looking at it to avoid having to eyeball him. She was a grown woman, but a dad's judgement was always difficult, and she hated, absolutely hated, even the thought that she might need his help.

"Come on, spit it out. I am your dad for crying out loud. Lousy dad or not, I am still it and I care about you. I know it must be important as it has been a while and the only price I will put on my help is that I get your mobile number, so we can keep in some kind of touch. That's my cards on the table, now it is your turn." He lent back in his chair, content that he had delivered his terms so early and now ready to hear whatever trouble she was in. Another gulp of water and she began.

"Of course we should swap numbers as it's ridiculous we don't have a way of speaking to each other. Bet you can't text," he held up a massive hand,
"Neither would you with these fingers." Both supped a bit more as they started to relax into each other's company.
"Before I tell you what's going on and what I MIGHT need from you, you have to promise to not get involved unless I say so and only do what we agree. Can you do that?" He cocked his head to one side, as if considering this, and after a brief pause gave a half nod. Then she told him what had happened, only leaving out the bit about her and Rich. She did not need his approval of any partner, be it a one night stand or anything more serious. Introducing the unexpected complication of Rich at this point would only be a distraction for her dad.

Once she had finished with the tale so far, she reached for her drink and he took his time to process it all.
"I am still not sure what you want from me."
"If the need arises, I MIGHT want to use your name, as it could at least stall them a bit. Then if they get heavy with me, I MIGHT need you to lend a bit of muscle to the situation. That will be a last resort and only if the kids are in any sort of danger. I am getting ahead of myself, as all they are asking at the minute is for me to take a dive

and earn them a few quid, but I am sure things can get out of hand on these deals. I can't have any harm come to the kids." She looked at his leathery face, searching for a clue as to what he was thinking, but he was giving nothing away. Up went the pint glass and the remainder of the drink disappeared down his throat.

"We both know this is more my world than yours and because of that you should let me tell you the way to sort it." She opened her mouth to put a stop to his train of thought, but he held up a hand with the palm facing her.

"No; no. You hear me out. If it was down to me I would pay Russ a little visit and he would know that if he did not leave you alone, his two useless sons would be on my Christmas shopping list, so to speak. Then we would see just how big his balls are. But, it is not down to me and you have made that very clear with all the 'MIGHTS' you keep throwing my way, so I will gladly go along with your plan for now. However, if anything happens to you or my grandkids, then I deal with it in my way." He said this in a way that was not seeking agreement or approval. It was a done deal, like it or not.

For all his brash tough exterior, Dog was no different to other men. He desperately wanted to be close to his family, see his grandkids more and all that goes with it. He had wanted to pick up the phone on so many occasions and beg Donna to let him back into her life, but he could not get beyond the weakness of it. Plus, the thought that she might just say no. So, he had carried on and whilst he was not exactly lonely, his many girlfriends over the years had provided comfort and affection, but too often they were more about someone being there and of course, sex. Not the same as family though. He did not like the plan, even though he understood it, and his blood was boiling at Russ and particularly at those prat sons of his. They had got Donna involved in all this. See how it plays out and cause some pain and grief if necessary. Do anything stupid here and it was as good as saying good-bye to any chance of getting closer to the kids. At his advancing years, it was not worth putting that in jeopardy.

"You have turned out alright Donna, you seem pretty switched on."
"Obviously that's no thanks to you, father," she gave him a big grin and he playfully raised the back of his hand.
"How's the boxing going? If you get over this crap, have you got a chance of making some serious money?" She looked at him quizzically for a second and he realised what she was thinking.
"I don't want your bleeding money, you stupid mare. I'm interested." He seemed genuine enough and she did know that whilst he was not minted, he was not short of a quid or two.
"Who knows. PD has taught me loads and I have a decent dig in my right, but it's all on the night. Not sure how much money is really on offer in girls boxing, but for now it is my best shot at giving the kids the life I want for them. I will take it as far

as I can and decide what to do from there."

"Could you box?" she asked. He let out a throaty chuckle,
"Hah, no, not really. Being a scrapper on the street is very different to rules and referees and all that stuff. I chose a different sort of fighting and it has served me alright I guess."
"Well, it seems I inherited something from you as I doubt I got it from mum." He was enjoying the chat.
"Fact is, I am sure your upbringing has played a part in your ability to take care of yourself and you have both me and your mum to 'not' thank for that. I would rather you were a doctor or lawyer, but I suppose I can accept being world champion as a poor substitute."
"Oh yeah, I remember now you were always keen for me to be a.... doctor!"

"Sorry dad, it's a flying stop as I need to get back for the kids, so I will be on my way soon." He looked deep into his empty glass.
"I could come with you and see the little ones," he still has not looked up.
"Let's play it cool for now dad. Give me your phone," he reached into his pocket and obediently handed it over.
"Well unlock it then," she said impatiently.
"Your birthday," he said quietly as he continued staring at the remnants of his drink and thumbing the side of the glass. She felt a slight lump in her throat and immediately fought it.
"You sly old dog. You must have played this moment out in advance and I have to say that was impressive, but not good enough to trick your own kin." Expertly, with her fingers a blur, she had added her name to his contacts.
"It's always been your birthday," and still his eyes had not left the glass. Shit, she thought.
"Listen, you stupid old sod, we have made a start and even though I was pretty desperate when I called, I am really pleased to have met up. Who knows what will happen from here, as long as you do not fuck it all up. You have my number, so call me as and when you need to, or of course, when you want to. Just not in the evenings as I'm busy sorting the kids. You will get to catch up with them soon enough, but right now I have got more than enough going on without introducing them to 'grandad'."
"Don't you want my number?"
"I have it; sent myself a text from your phone. I'm off, and dad......thanks." She squeezed his shoulder and was gone.

"You silly old twot," he said to himself out loud. How could anything be more important than keeping her and the family closer to him? Circumstances could partly be blamed, but more recently it had been the debilitating effect of his stupid pride preventing him from making the call. Then there was the fear of her rejecting any attempt he might make to play a part in her and his grandchildren's lives. To all the other emotions he was now feeling, guilt was added in, because those wankers would not have messed with Donna if they had known he was related to her. Then he began asking himself if he had the discipline not to do something bad to every one of those Tomkins.

As he looked up she was coming back. "By the way, hair gel suits you." Big grin, she playfully flung her hair back and ran her fingers through it in an exaggerated way and was gone again.

CHAPTER 14.

"There are better people in the world, do not let the worst do the worst to you, you deserve the best in life." — Michael Bassey Johnson.

Rich was lying face down on the bed and Donna was lying on him stroking his back; he loved the feel of her next to him. He had been with plenty of girls, but this one, this one was so different. All those soppy films on TV where the leading man says, 'I just knew', and all that crap, well 'all that crap' was happening to him. He thought about her constantly and hated not being with her. When he saw her, he was like a little puppy, as he could not hide how pleased he was to see her. The simple truth was he didn't know why, and he could not stop it. Perhaps there is a special someone out there for everyone? He had never felt more content with anyone. So now that he had found this gorgeous, brilliant, funny girl, why the hell was there so much rubbish attached to it?

"Why could you not be ugly?"
"Surely one ugly person in any relationship is enough."
"Oh yeah, that from a boxer with a bit more than a hint of cauliflower ears...."
Whack to the back of the head.

"Rich?"
"What?" She propped herself up on one elbow, "Before your messing about, I said, so what are we going to do?"
Without moving at all he said,
"I have been thinking about that and there seems only one answer." Silence. Donna pokes a finger into his ribs. He jolts a bit, but continues as motionless as possible. "Well?"
"I think our best plan is to stay here and hope it all goes away."
"Then you are fucking useless." With that she gets up angrily and walks away from the bed.
"No sugar in mine," he can't contain how pleased he is with himself at this and opens one eye to see a plastic water bottle heading his way. He just about dodges it and sits up.
"Violence is never the answer," he says in a Ladyship voice. She's close to cracking and he knows it.
"Also, I love you. I really love you." She gets back in bed and they cuddle up and lay

in each other's arms.

"I just don't know what to do babe, you know where I'm from and I am not sure I can tell my dad it's all off, because I have got hooked up with the cash prize of the whole thing." She nips him twice quite hard.
"Hey! That hurt. What was that for anyway?"
"Do not call me babe and do not refer to me as a cash prize," she said monotone.
"That's really helpful of you. Nipping is not the answer either. Now where was I, that's right, I was discussing you as the cash.... cow!" He flinched immediately, shuffled away from her and tried to protect as many exposed parts as possible. She did not react at all, she just looked around the room as though she had lost something. Through his fingers he asked, "What are you doing?" Without stopping her scan of the room, she said, "Just wondering where I put that knuckle duster......" Then her mood got serious.

"Unless you have got some brilliant new suggestion, it seems quite simple to me Rich, you either tell your dad or give me up." She hugged him tight and then began to roll away.
"Donna, for the first time in my life I know what it feels like to be scared of my dad. I have had hidings off him over the years, but if he gets wind of this, then who knows what he will do to me and more importantly, to you. However, above that fear is the simple fact that I am not sure how I could carry on without you in my life. We may have only recently got to know each other, but it's just so right. Here is what I think. You go ahead with the fight, take the loss and then we go public in a few months' time, as if we have only just got together. You and the kids are left alone, dad knows nothing about any of this and we get to build a life together." He knew it was not perfect, but it was not bad and with a look-how-clever-I-am expression, he drew his gaze to hers to see if he was getting any sort of positive vibes from her. When he could not wait any longer, he said, "So, what do you think?"

"I think..............you should grow a pair." She was controlled, but angry. "You dragged me into this mess and your solution involves me risking my career whilst you carry on as normal, no doubt meeting up in secret for a leg over every so often, and then perhaps we can go public. Hhhhhmmmm........you can go fuck yourself."

"Donna, my suggestion is not genius I know, but it is the best I've got; we've got, as far as I know. Yes, this is all my stupid fault, but I can't turn back time so there's no point you pinning all hopes for a solution on me. We are way beyond that. Letting you go is not an option for me, so we need to come up with something and fast."

Donna got up and sat in a chair, putting her head in her hands as she contemplated what Rich had said. She had really fallen for him, but even so she was still angry at him for involving her in this. Problem being, she was having trouble seeing beyond it being up to him to resolve what he had caused.

"Rich, it's clear how I feel about you and I hope, really hope, that we get to take it on after this is all out of the way. However, that might be never, as I imagine your old man is not the forgive and forget type and who knows, he might think I can earn him a few more quid if this goes well for him. Above my feelings for you, is the welfare of those two kids and I will not let them get hurt. It's too early in us being together for you to have any idea of what I am capable of, but where they are concerned it's pretty limitless. You are right, we do need to think of a way out and make no bones about it, I have been pinning that massively on you for obvious reasons. But I will get past that and see if there is a way to unpick this mess. I don't think too straight when we are together, so let's take a break for a couple of days and then see where our thinking is at."

Rich was sitting up. "I will hate not seeing you, but if that is what it takes then so be it. One thing you should know. I regret, so much, getting you involved in my sordid world and bringing all this shite your way. However, if I hadn't, I wouldn't have met you. I know it does not excuse anything and I also know it makes me extremely selfish, but Christ I'm pleased I found you. We have to find a way, or we could be facing the biggest regret of all."

Donna lifted her head slightly, so that her eyes were peering over her fingers and said, "That was lovely, thank you." They got up and hugged each other very tightly for a while and as they released he said, "As we're not going to see each other for a while, how about a quick shag to be going on with...." She released him and was about to launch into a few well placed thumps, when she saw the cheeky sparkle in his eyes. "Go on then, I'm sure I can spare 40 seconds for you. Anyway, if I wear it out a bit perhaps, just perhaps, you can stop thinking with it and who knows, you might be able to do something about our longer term future."

Even though they were often engaged in serious conversations, when they were together it was easy for them to somehow block out those sobering issues and just enjoy being with each other. The banter was a part of it and due to their personalities, it was never far away. Did it seem wrong that whilst the lives of so many innocent people could be affected by what they did or did not do, they still found time to mess about in meaningless, verbal ripostes and play fighting? It did not seem wrong to them, it just did not seem anything. Like many new couples getting to know each other, it provided the distraction they needed from the trials and tribulations of everyday life. Without planning it, or thinking too much about it, they were finding a way to let their burgeoning love have a fair shake at developing into something magical. If young love let problems stop couples growing into each other, then there would be very little real love in this world.

CHAPTER 15.

"I know you think I'm crazy. Maybe that's because I am. About life, about this moment, about you." — Crystal Woods.

Layla and Donna were very close and pretty much knew each other's lives inside out, so if she were to confide in anyone it would be Layla. Even though almost everything was a joke to Layla, she was switched on and sensible when it was needed. What Donna needed most of all was to tell someone, other than Rich, about what was happening as it was quite obviously playing on her mind constantly. She called Layla round for a coffee and after a few giggles about nothing much, Donna started to update her mate on what was occurring.

"You know about the Tomkins and the fight and all that, well there have been developments." She was taking her time, because even to her it was madness, so she wanted to get her delivery spot on.
"Do not tell me you have jumped the old bones of Russ Tomkins," Layla blurted out in the way people do when it feels a quip will make the situation less awkward.
"No! But you are nearer than you might think." She gulped some of the coffee she had been staring at.
"Who then; Chan???"
"Do not judge me..."
"Too late, who?" The coffee mug was held in both hands and she seemed to use it to steady herself.
"Well, I might just have somehow got friendly with one of his sons; Rich is his name."

Layla stood up, placed both hands flat on the worktop and stared out of the kitchen window.
"When you say friendly, how 'friendly'?" Donna looked at the back of her mate's head.
"If I was to say I think he's the one, would that help you understand what's going on?" Layla spun round and looked at Donna, who for the first time in as long as she could recall, looked sheepish and vulnerable.
"Oh Donna, come here." Donna buried her face into Layla and wrapped her arms round her waist. She held her very tight.
"What do you want to hear from me?" They release each other, and Donna sits down

again.
"Shall we begin with you getting your thoughts off your chest about what I've done, so then we can chat properly?"
"I thought you would never ask. You stupid cow! Not content with your gob and fists getting you in trouble, now you have decided to enlist the rest of your body. You could not write this stuff. You are a stupid woman."

Donna took it all and said, "That's twice I have been called a cow today." She grabbed Layla's hand.

"Layla, he's good looking, really good looking, believe it or not he is kind to me, charming, funny and in any other situation you would have said he was so right for me. He will take on the kids too." Layla could see how bad Donna had got it for this guy. "Do you have any idea how to make it work, because if not, there is more pain coming your way than you have ever felt in the ring? By the way, apart from the fact that he has fucked up your already fucked up life even more, he sounds great. But no, I am not interested in hooking up with his brother!"

"Rich thinks I should take the fall, keep us quiet and then we 'come out' as a couple in a few months' time."
"Allowing for the fact that you are besotted with him, can I just say......fucker!" With that Layla returns to the table and sits down.
"That's what I said, but on reflection what else is there to do? I'm in a shit situation however you look at it, but for me and the kids it could turn out to be the best way out of this." Layla reached and grabbed both her friend's hands. "As you know, people usually do this as a show of affection, but I'm doing it, so you can't hit me." They grinned. "You are not going to like this. It's all cosy thinking, but, and it's a big but, what happens if Russ doesn't want his little boy mixing with the likes of you. Had you thought of that?" She had. "Then the only difference from where I was, will be that I have had a very decent shag for a few months."

"So, go with his plan then, keep him on the QT, take a dive and then see if life can be dreamy with Mr. Right down the line. If not, can we cut his balls off?"

"There is something else." Layla, let go of Donna's hands, "I am not sure how you can top what you have already told me, but I bet you are about to have a real go. You are not up the duff are you?"

"No, how stupid do you think I am?" No words needed as Layla tilts her head towards Donna and raises her eyebrows. Donna ignores this and carries on.

"The kids are my main concern and I am not sure I can control everything that will happen with Russ and his crew going forward, because he's a gangster for fuck's sake. So, to do what I can to make sure they are protected no matter what comes our way, I have told dad about what's going on. He's only there if I need him and he has agreed to that, but I felt I had to do something."

A nervous reflex took hold, as Layla scratches her head and then looks Donna in the eye. "In what way does throwing the most dangerous man we probably know, based on what you have told me, into this mix, make life safer for the kids?" Donna did not blink. "He is not a danger to me or the kids and I am having to think like they do. If not, Russ will just roll over me without a second thought. With dad in the picture he will at least have second thoughts, as he will know what he is capable of."

"Donna, I hope you are right about this. Are you certain he will listen to you, as he has always seemed a bit 'lone wolf' from what you have said? With what is at stake you have got to be the one who decides what happens."
"I have thought about that and when I met up with him it was obvious he wants to be a granddad in more than just name. I am banking on him not risking that by doing anything stupid. It was good to see him, actually far better than I had imagined, and knowing I have him in the background has made me feel more able to deal with it all, strange though that may seem. If I do let the leash off, that is when I will not be able to control him and then I may well rue his involvement, as Rich could be in serious bother."

Layla clasped her hands together, "So, daddy dear does not know about the new boyfriend then?" Donna bristled, "No, and I do not need permission or approval from him for who I choose to see. The kid's safety is my main concern, my only concern, and once I am satisfied they will be OK, then I will think more about my relationships with dad and Rich. Telling him now was going to make it all even more complicated than it already is. That joyous task will have to wait. By the way, if they know we are friends they could try to involve you at some point, so take care. Think about where you go and what you do and stay vigilant."

"Well, that is just fucking brilliant. Donna, forget anything I may have said and make sure your dad knows who I am and what a terrific friend to you I have been. As you say, just in case."

CHAPTER 16.

It takes a certain type of man to become a boxer, to fight for a living. To be able to have the confidence to hit another man, to control your fears. You must overcome the physical aspect and believe in the art, the discipline of the sport. You need to study. You need to be smart. – Anthony Joshua.

Chan arrived outside his home late afternoon, as was mostly the case, because he could then get some grub, relax a little and be ready for accompanying Russ wherever he was going that evening. It was his few moments of tranquility in an otherwise tiring day, because his job was to protect the boss. That meant getting in the way of any idiot stupid enough to have a go or being scary enough to make sure that did not happen. Those who did throw a punch at Russ were desperate men who Russ had pushed to the point of no return or had hurt them very badly financially. Chan had ethics and he was not always proud of what he was involved in, but his line of work paid well. His sheer size and bulk prevented him having to fly into action very often. On the occasions it had been necessary, everyone knew what a mistake it was. Chan was not only big, but very skilled. He had studied boxing, Karate, Brazilian Jujitsu and some other forms of fighting or self-protection, depending on how you looked at it, and to say he could handle himself was one hell of an understatement. Ethics or not he needed to live and he was paid handsomely by Russ. As long as the business they were involved in did not get too out of control, he would stick with it for a while.

Everyone seemed to know of Chan, either through his attendance at gyms, martial arts classes or through his association with Russ. However, he was also really liked. If you faced him in a 'proper' contest, then the minute it was over it was forgotten. Even in the day job he tried to be a decent bloke, as much as that was possible. Rather than give everyone who crossed Russ a pasting, he talked to them first and did all he could to reason with them. Some minders enjoyed hurting people and took every opportunity to do so. But what did that prove? That was not the Chan way.

Pay up, or do what Russ was asking of you, and whether you happened to find his request unpalatable or not, Chan was not there to discuss the pros and cons. He was there to enforce the message. If you got a 'slap' from Chan it was quick, it hurt, and you probably deserved it for not taking the hint that to proceed would not be good for your health. It was rare that the slap was not enough, but if he had to cause pain he would. Because he gave people a chance to avoid this, he did not feel bad when he dished a real beating out. But that was as far as he would go. If Russ wanted someone to disappear he had other resources to make that happen.

As he neared his front door, he stopped. Instinct in this game was crucial to remaining safe and he felt a certain unease.
"Hi Chan. Thought we should talk." Jeez, it was Dog. He knew of him, because it was his job to know the local faces, and whilst they were on nodding terms, they were far from mates.
"I do not like people confronting me outside my own house, so let's do this some other time." Dog stood directly in front of him,
"Nope. Let's do it now." Chan just wanted his down time, so he let out a big sigh.
"Man, if this is some macho crap you are making a big mistake." Dog did not flinch.
"The boxing girl your boss is attempting to fuck over is my daughter."
Silence.
"What's that got to do with you being here?" Dog relaxed his stature a bit and said,
"That macho crap you talked about, well could be we are head on for it, so I thought I would see myself close up what you were all about. I am also giving you a chance to get out of the way. You are impressive and I hear about how well you can handle yourself, BUT do not for a second think you will get in my way if my family is involved. You won't. Do you know much about me?" Chan thought for a second or two.
"Enough. I work for Russ and he pays me to do what he asks and as you can imagine I have to deal with unhappy people quite a bit of the time. Some of them are tough guys like you and that's where I really earn my keep. Whatever I feel about you or your daughter will not matter if you get in the way of me doing my job. We clear?"

"I think we are both clear on where each other stands, and....... I know where you live." Chan flinched a bit as he was not used to being threatened.
"Don't like that, do you? Well, get used to being the prey if this gets messy. By the way, if my girl gets hurt I will come for you after I settle the score with the boys who got her into this, and you know they won't cause me to even break stride. Then I will pay Russ a surprise visit. Not sure what your employment situation or medical wellbeing will be then." Dog, points at Chan. "Actually, I have caused you a problem, haven't I? If you tell Russ about our little chat, he will wonder why you did not have a go. Or do you not tell him, but then what about if he finds out? Either way, he might lose some trust in you."

Chan knows he is right and just as the thought of sorting this right here and now flies into his mind, Dog flashes a wooden truncheon, with what appeared to be nails sticking out of it. "One step ahead of you. You are not stupid enough to take me and this on, so let's forget all about you even trying. Take care how deep you get into this Chan, because I will kill anyone who harms my girl, or her family, and you can bet that includes you. In case you didn't hear me, I said KILL. Bypass A & E and straight to the morgue. Be seeing you." Dog then backs away carefully and is soon gone.

Chan felt angry, and that did not happen very often. He was now in a predicament. Not only that, his quiet time had been shot to pieces as he would be consumed with this now. Whether Dog was tooled up or not, he should have taken him out there and then. However, Dog had caught him on the hop and just like when Chan himself stood in front of people, this too was a force to be reckoned with. The man, the reputation, tooled up and with the emotion of his daughter getting caught up in this matter, all made for a less than straight forward day at the office. After much brain churning, he decided to keep the meeting to himself for now. However, he could not work out why this man known for his violence was just talking about what he would do and not doing it. Chan liked life simple. This was anything but.

* * *

"Talk me through where we are at, with the fight that bitch is helping us with." Russ was holding court with Rich and Dean in his office. It could almost have been a sales meeting from any business up and down the land, with Russ as the regional director talking to his sales managers. He wanted to know the profit projections, where the money was being taken and how they could increase their take. Dean ran through the likely outcome of the betting they had planned and £20k was looking very realistic. He hoped Russ would be pleased, but knew he would be expecting more, as always.

"What's our share of the ticket sales? Please tell me we have covered that?"

Dean shuffled in his seat. "When we ran the plan by you it was about the betting and that was all."

"Dean, this was also about you starting to show me that you could take over the business before I reach 150, so I presumed you would be seeing how you could maximise the profit from all sources. Get on it and the same for the bar and grub sales. Can you do that yourself or do you need Chan?" Dean felt pissed off for being made to look a prat by Russ and also for not thinking about the other ways to generate cash himself. "I will sort it."

During this exchange Rich kept quiet as he was finding it really uncomfortable to hear Russ call Donna a bitch. He wanted to tell him to shut up and come clean about what was going on. But, he didn't. In part, this was because Donna would need to know before he did this, but mostly he knew he was being a coward. That did not sit well with him at all. Russ was well aware Rich was not being his normal self and threw a dig at him.

"What's the matter with you, someone stole your favourite doll or something?" He grinned at himself and winked at Dean to show how pleased he was with his wit. "Why do you make out we are girls when you say stuff like that? Pisses me right off." Rich regretted the outburst immediately. He attempted to recover the situation. "Sorry dad, I know you are messing with us. I'm fine, just not feeling totally with it at present. I will go with Deano and we'll let you know how we get on with the extra income."

He went to make a move and was only too conscious of his brother staring at him and his dad staring, into him. Russ barked at him, "Sit the fuck down." He then took time to compose himself. "I am your dad and will speak to you however I want to. As you both missed a chance here, then I think you are lucky I use humour instead of a bollicking. I love you dearly, but come it with me like that again and we will find out how much of a man you are. You drive the car you do, wear those designer clothes and have this easy life, all down to me. So rather than being pissed off at a little comment that got under your skin, I suggest you remember who is responsible for the life you enjoy. Be careful Rich. Think before you speak, because next time I will act before I think. Now get out, the pair of you."

Once out of earshot of Russ, Dean grabbed his brother by the arm, "What the fuck was that about? You biting back at dad, I mean what came over you?" Rich shrugged the arm off him and looked at Dean. "It's nothing, leave it be. Like I said, I'm just not feeling myself that's all." Dean pushed him hard in the chest with one hand, "Well, that's all fine and dandy, but you are not fucking things up and taking me down with you. Next time you fancy making a death wish with dad, just do it when you are on your own." Rich swiped the hand away, "Listen you idiot, I did not plan to say anything, it just came out. You are not dad, so quit playing this hard man with me unless you think the most sensible thing we can do is throw a few punches and see who comes out on top. I'm sure dad will be super pissed if we do."

They stepped away from each other and as Dean straightened his tie, he said, "This was about us taking on more of the business, so get your brain in gear from now on, because we need each other to make that happen. Now let's make a few visits and give the old fella something to smile about." Despite wanting it so bad for so long, at the present time, taking over the business was not a priority for Rich. His head was full to bursting with all that was going on. Today, it had leaked out a bit. His feelings for Donna raging against his loyalty to his dad and brother, even more heightened by Dean being his best mate; but how could he tell him? Doing so would push Dean into a position where he had to choose between dad and brother, and that was not fair.

He decided to speak to Donna later, as that would cheer his spirits. For the rest of the day he would concentrate on squeezing the promoters of the fight, and the bar manager, for a share of their takings. In return he would offer a no damage to person or environment agreement. That way, hopefully no-one would ask any more questions about his being off-colour. His head was wracking at trying to find a way he could square everything off, without losing Donna or falling out with Russ and Dean. It had completely taken over and yet he was nowhere near cracking this code. He normally slept like a log, but last night he had tossed and turned. His sluggishness of thought showed that was catching up with him too. He got himself together, pulled at his shirt collar and ran his hand through his hair. I just hope she does not do anything silly, he thought to himself.

* * *

For once there was no pretence, no façade with Russ. He thumped the desk hard and pulled at his silk tie and ripped the top button of his shirt open. His face was red, his veins popping, and he was decidedly dishevelled. Uncharacteristically that did not seem to be of any importance to him, as his mind whirred over what had just happened. That was not like Rich, but he had noticed he was distant more and more of late and today was the final straw. Everyone loved his jokes and his wise cracks so why had Rich gone off on one? He tried to think back to anything he had said before that to give him a clue. No, nothing. Anything different happened at work? Again, nothing sprung to mind. They would all be out together for the fight tomorrow, so perhaps a few bevvies would regroup them and if not, he would have it out with him the day after. Ungrateful little sod, he thought.

What on earth was going on? There was Rich acting up and earlier on Chan had been out of character when he dealt with one of the 'tenants' who wanted to give Russ a piece of his mind. The normal think-about-it whisper in the ear had been replaced with a solid and devastating blow to the stomach, swiftly followed with a vice like grip on this poor bastard's throat until he changed colour. Then he was thrown to the floor in a way that caused his head to bounce off the concrete with a sickening crunch. He asked Chan about it once they were back in the car and all he said was, "Every so often people need to know who they are dealing with or liberties will be taken." The upside was, word would get around and there would be no trouble getting everyone to pay on time for the foreseeable future. Still, the way he acted and the way he justified his actions was not Chan.

Was it a coincidence they had both shown a different side to their character on the same day, or had he missed something. He could not think of anything that would link their unusual displays, no matter how long and hard he thought. He left his office and found Chan in one of the outer rooms eating, like normal. This time on a Blueberry Yoghurt protein bar. "Do you know of anything to do with Rich that I should know about?" The question was hard and true, and Russ would know if Chan was lying; that was his forte. "No boss." No emotion, no reaction at all, he was re-assured that Chan knew nothing. As he made his way back to his office, his train of thought was leading him away from where the answer would come and now he was wondering if Chan was being tempted by a competitor; what else could it be?

He turned on his heels and headed back to Chan, striking whilst the iron was still hot was the Russ way. "If you do choose to leave my employment, you can only do so if you find a replacement. Understand?" Chan was puzzled at this outburst aimed his way, but soon this gave way to irritation. "Boss, if you want me to leave just say so, because we both know I can find similar employment elsewhere. I am here because I choose to be here. I do not like games, so say if you want someone else to look after you." The response stoked Russ out of his verbal assault, here he was pissing off the best minder there is and for no good reason. "Chan, I'm sorry. I put two and two together and made five. I thought you might have been looking elsewhere, but as long as you are happy with me, then let's not mention it again." Chan, chewed on the remnants of the protein bar and simply said, "I did not mention it; you did."

Russ made his way back to his office, annoyed that he had made a fool of himself with Chan and been rightly told so by the man mountain, with appropriate force as per his more usual style. Hopefully, things would soon be back to normal, but if this kept up he was having it out with Rich and Chan next week. Until then, he would do his best to leave it alone.

Russ manoeuvred his chunky fingers to fix his top button, aligned his tie and resumed his ultra-executive appearance. He sat down in his lovely chair and steepled his fingers. The niggling in his brain was still there though and it crossed his mind, was he getting too old for the game he was in? Was he missing things that were happening? He had been a fighter all his life and that was not about to change, so perhaps he needed to show everyone that he still had what it takes to be the master of his streets. His thoughts reflected on what Chan had done earlier, when he lashed out, and perhaps that was the way. He would choose his moment and then one or more people who weren't in line, or who were pushing it to the line, would remember why he was the feared man he was. He rocked back the chair and began to think of opportunities to demonstrate he still had it.

CHAPTER 17.

"It's just a job. Grass grows, birds fly, waves pound the sand. I beat people up." - Muhammad Ali.

A dressing room on fight night is just so gladiatorial, because the danger is real and the excitement so palpable. Some boxers may say they do not think about the dangers, but in truth it is there somewhere, no matter how well hidden. The last instruction from the referee is always, 'Protect yourself at all times', which is not the same as, 'Throw your best punches at all times'. For all the matches that end up with no lasting damage, the ones where death or life changing injuries had been involved were sure to make massive headlines, so every boxer and spectator knew what could happen. So why do it? Same reason as Donna. Probably the best route to a better life or maybe, for some, the best route out of the life they were destined for. Involvement in a sport where getting punched regularly is part and parcel may not be a terrific choice, but if the alternative is getting kicked by the system for the rest of your life, then the choice becomes far more appealing.

Donna had shared on some previous occasions, but tonight a big room had been partitioned off into 6 smaller rooms and whilst she could hear the others going through their pre-match routines, she was pleased she had some privacy. At this level there is not a big entourage firing you up, telling you how great you are and any other kind of arse licking some high profile boxers require. Just her and PD and that's how she liked it. She could think, prepare and get as physically and mentally ready as possible. PD knew she did not need to get pumped up as her style required her to be in control of her faculties. Her approach was not to blow her opponent away in the first few seconds, but to take her opportunities, which she generated through methodically wearing them down. He joked, talked tactics, rubbished her choice of music and generally kept things very light, but focused. It worked for her and despite being very different to every other pre-fight dressing room he had been in, he enjoyed it.

PD was trying to carry on as normal in how he prepped Donna for the fight and so he taped her hands, got her to do some shadow boxing and then unleash a few punches into his pads, but it was halfhearted and they both knew it. "Come on you soppy old git, get me ready as you would for a world title bout. I may be taking a fall, but before I do, that stupid cow is going to taste her own blood and I want to be warmed up when the bell goes." As many men do in situations over which they have little or no control, PD was acting a bit sulky, so Donna playfully jabbed him in the belly. He made some weird noise, having been caught off guard. Then he saw the funny side, letting out a small bark of a laugh.

"Every time you punch her, see Russ and take your aggro out on him through her. Motivational speech over."
"Are you for real? I'm meant to lose and if I keep seeing his face, I will beat the living daylights out of her."
"You're right. See my face then."
"Same result I fear."
"Ha. I'm useless at everything tonight, can't even come up with a decent pep talk. Listen, once we get this panto out of the way I will do all I can to get you back on track with your career; I promise you that." Donna felt a tear coming and swallowed to compose herself. The kids, PD, her dad, they were all involved to greater or lesser degrees and she hated that.

"Sulky and soppy is not a great combination and thank fuck it isn't a big fight or my head would be all over the place. What happens after tonight we'll worry about later, but for now I have got a job to do; or not!." Hers was the third fight on the undercard, of some regional match between two local middleweights, and as the second bout was underway she could be called fairly soon. To keep warm and prepared, she did some gentle skipping with her iPod thumping out Nickelback's 'Rock Star', through her headphones. She always played it on fight nights and tonight would be no different as she was determined to get herself in the zone. She would enter the ring looking primed, with sweat dripping and grease protecting her eyes, ready to go to work.

There was a knock on the door and one of the events team entered in the same movement. "Fights just finished, so be ready in 2." Then they were gone. "PD. I hate, fucking hate, boxing." She fought back the tears, angry tears, as she hissed this out in his direction. "I know," he looked as though he was about to offer a few words to sort her head out. "But you are shite at everything else," he somehow kept a straight face. Just as the realisation of what he was saying shone through the mist, he added, "Mind you, we get a chance to find out if diving is a talent tonight." He stepped back, and his grin stretched wide. How did he know just what to say in such moments? She stepped into his space and hugged him; a heartfelt hug he could feel the intensity of. She let go, looked up and concentrated on her breathing to collect her thoughts, as different tears were welling up now. "Anyhow, you be careful old man, because I have a stack of energy and anger to get rid of tonight and if I do not satisfy it on her, I might well turn to you when we get back in here."

"Get yourself ready and stop all this talk of satisfying me please. There are loads ahead of you in the queue and anyway.......... you will be all sweaty." They both knew this banter was no way to prepare for a fight, but for this night it was the best way to get through it. "Ewww, PD enough of that." Then they looked at each other and he said, "Let's just get this fucking night over and done with," and pushed her towards the door. She became very aware of the noise in the Hall as she exited the changing room. All the talking, drunken shouts, laughing and small roars of combined voices, for what reason she would have no way of knowing. She felt flat, but on auto pilot she went through all the normal steps of shrugging her shoulders round and round and throwing a few jabs and crosses as she moved through the crowd on her way to the ring. She noticed many of the punters weren't taking any interest in anything other than their drink or the conversation they were taking part in.

Her opponent was already in the ring and pacing around as Donna firmly placed her right foot on the steps that led to the ring. She bopped down through the ropes and eyed her foe. She was half cast by the look of her and carrying some weight around the middle. Her hair was pulled back tightly on top and the sides of her head were shaved, revealing weird little stumpy ears. She clearly liked the odd tattoo and Donna realised how relaxed she was feeling, because rather than running through the fight plan in her head, she was trying to make out what animal that was on the forearm. It was a big cat of some sort, with the head of a snake and it was done by a shit artist; all blurry lines with dodgy looking colours.

Donna had heard of her from the local fight scene, but she was a 'turn up and have a go girl' who every so often got lucky with her big right hand. She was never expected to step her career up above this local tournament level. Mind you, after tonight, will I? Along with the pacing, she was staring at Donna and imitating all that macho crap by pointing her glove and shouting, "I am going to beat you so bad. I am going to hurt you bitch." Donna loved all that normally, as it fired her up just that bit more, but tonight she was indifferent to it. Just her luck, here she was in the ring with someone who had seen one too many Rocky films and was giving it the full vocals, she would normally feed off. She felt nothing. She went through the motions of chucking a few jabs at some imaginary person and skipping from one foot to the other. She hated that people had paid money for tonight and were not going to see a show from her bout. Perhaps all the bouts tonight were rigged?

Donna glanced out at the horde and saw Russ and his boys. They were clearly enjoying their entertainment so far, which they watched from a table right at the front. All three were suited up and acting like they owned the place, which to be fair they probably did! Russ was waiting for Donna to look their way and as she did, he looked straight at her and grinned. He gave her a wink to say, 'be a good girl', and equally, but far more annoyingly, 'you are mine'. She received the bat of his eye, accompanied by a half nod and realised how much age gap there was between them. He's doing the type of wink old men do to young children in my direction! She looked right back at him and pretended to be sick, which by his reaction he did not appreciate very much. His grin disappeared. Rich saw the exchanges and frowned at

Donna and then grabbed his dad's attention with a clink of his glass to indicate he should drink up. Russ accepted the bait and he loosened up again as he felt the soothing heat of his whiskey.

Dean observed the eye contact between Rich and this girl. He shuffled uncomfortably in his seat. "Rich, can I see you for a minute?" The look on his brother's face told him Dean had got a right grump about something. Russ saw a chance to jibe his son, "Can't you go to the toilet on your own Dean? Need someone to hold it for you?" He liked to be loud in such moments and he cast his eyes beyond his own table to see who else had enjoyed his quip. He let loose a throaty laugh, but his sons weren't with him at all. No reaction, he was not used to that.
"What the fuck's going on?"
"Nothing dad, relax," said Rich.
"We'll grab another drink and be back to see the dosh rain down on us."

"So?" Once out of ear shot of his dad, Dean turned on his brother, determined to know what the score was.
"So, so what? What's got to you?" Rich did his best to control his gestures, but knew he was coming across a bit shifty and far from his normal self. Dean had no intention of letting it go.
"I spend an awful lot of time with you bruv and whilst you might be blessed with more grey matter than me, that does not mean I'm completely stupid. Now, I saw you and that girl in the ring and how you looked at each other. I also know that you haven't been spending so much time on the business as you used to. Add in the fact that when you are at work, you might as well not be, and I think I have clocked something I do not like. Something the old man will rip your nuts off for, if I'm right. Again, I'm asking. So?"

"Deano, me and you are solid - always will be. Just leave this be, because right now I do not need you poking a stick at it." Rich saw Dean was going to continue his thoughts on what he would consider his brother's stupidity, so he beat him to it. "Enough bro, I have told you; leave it." He slapped him on the top of his arm and headed for the bar. Dean could feel his head was spinning. Should I tell dad, should I have another go at getting Rich to see sense, although by the last exchange that was unlikely. There they were edging closer to taking over the business and now Rich had dipped it where he shouldn't and probably ballsed it up for both of them. What to do?

He knew he was not thinking straight at all. As was often the best policy when his head was all over the place, and most people's default position in difficult circumstances, he decided he would, do nothing.

I'll sit back down, give dad my best grin and down that whiskey and water in one hit, because I could do with a drink more than ever. The old man does not miss anything and a hit of Scotland's best might help me mask my thoughts.

He saw something in his brother's eyes that he had not seen before; maybe it's time to realise the need for me to consider, 'What if?'

Based on what had happened over the last few days, Russ had unconsciously engaged a more heightened sensitivity to all that was happening around him. He saw the worried look on Dean's face. So much for a spot of bonding at the fight, it was clear all was not good between Dean and Rich and he was going to have it out tomorrow.

Rich carried a tray with six drinks on it; a lager and whiskey chaser for each of them. "Funnily enough, there was no charge for these." Russ could sense Rich was trying too hard, as they rarely paid for a drink when out in their neighbourhood, so why was Rich making such a song and dance about it this time? He purposely watched for the eye contact between them. It was non-existent. The mood had turned frosty.

Something had irked Dean and yet Rich was playing the life and soul of the party in a way he had not for a while. Let's push this a bit, "Cheers lads. To a knock-out night for the Tomkins." Glasses were raised, clinked, but Russ got absolutely no eye contact from either of them. That's it, no more drink for me tonight after this round. I want to be totally in control of my senses, so I can observe and take in everything that happens around me. Someone will give me a clue as to what is going on as they get more and more ratted. Let's shake the tree again.

"Another toast lads. Normal service, will soon be restored." He got a reaction, just as he had assumed his comment would cause. Now, what has that revealed? Dean's display of shock and his expression clearly laid bare they were keeping something from him. Rich looked calmer, as always. Russ sensed he probably knew his dad was fishing, but even so he could see he was flustered. Was that fear he saw? He was just about to order them to meet him in a room at the back when the announcer grabbed the mic.

'Ladies and gentlemen, next on the undercard tonight is a lightweight bout, which is an eliminator for the Area Title, between two of the best female boxers we have locally. It is over ten rounds and we have three scoring judges; Mary Jones, Tom Shepless and Frank Graden.

First of all, we have Latrice 'Lights Out' Lindenberry, who weighed in at 9 stone 7 lbs. She brings a record of 12 fights, with 8 wins, including 7 by knock out. Give it up for Laaaaattttrrrriccccee. Latrice raised her arms above her head to acknowledge the crowd, but she kept up the stare she held on Donna. As she dropped her arms, she mouthed, 'Going down', and prodded her gloves at the floor of the ring. Donna smirked at the ridiculousness of it all.

Next, we have Donna 'Wham Bam' Wilbraham, who weighed in at 9 stone 6lb. She has had 9 fights, with no defeats and has won 8 by knock out. I give you Dooooomnnnnnnnnnaaaaaaaaaaa. Donna stepped one pace forward, waved one handed to the crowd and paced backwards to her corner. PD rinsed out the gumshield and offered it up to Donna, who opened her mouth and he put it firmly in place. He lent in close to her ear, "Do this, and let's be done with this." She nodded. It was not the most motivational speech ever, but it did not need to be. She looked across and Latrice's trainer was in her ear pumping her up and no doubt delivering some Rocky type pre-fight chat he had been memorising.

CHAPTER 18.

"Now I know why tigers eat their young." — Al Capone.

The referee called the boxers together and she was still running her mouth off. It was starting to grate on Donna. She had stayed calm all this while and in a normal fight she could have stuck to her routine and all this crap would fade into the background. But this was not a normal fight night and there was no routine for her to follow for when she was expected to lose. Even knowing it was not a good idea, Donna decided to get involved in the verbal slanging.

"Unless you want to regret tonight forever, I suggest you shut the fuck up." Latrice enjoyed the taunts as it fired her up and now Donna was joining in she knew she was getting to her.

"You will regret ever seeing me bitch and you won't see this baby of a right as it lands on your pig ugly face, because I'm too strong, too fast..........." The lips were moving, but Donna stopped even trying to make out what the words were. The ref intervened and began to tell them his final instructions ahead of the bout, when Donna suddenly felt something snap inside her head. All the frustrations about this whole charade spilled over. She could feel her anger simmering just below the surface. Rather than just getting on with what is nothing more than a stupid pantomime, why is this girl so intent on pissing me off. Her self-control dissolved as the fury took over and without any conscious direction, she lunged forward and pushed Latrice with a double fisted shove, straight in the chest. As if it was slow motion, Latrice tried to stay upright, but she was not in command of her legs, which had already begun their Bambi impression.

The room fell silent except for those who had not been watching, but gradually the awareness of something not being right seeped into every corner, swamping the drunken chatter. The attack was unexpected and caught Latrice off guard, however shock had been replaced by embarrassment. She glowered up in disbelief. Donna regained her composure to find the referee in her face, wagging his finger at her, all to a noisy backdrop of laughing and cheering as the patrons revelled in the bonus piece of theatre.

Once back on her feet, Latrice felt even more of a need to hurl a few comments

Donna's way, she knew she had to get back in the zone.
"Cheap shot bitch, you are right to be scared, I am going to.......," the ref knew to jump in quickly and get the fight back on track;
"You know the rules, so break when I say break and protect yourself at all times."

Donna held out her gloves in the time honoured tradition and Latrice, wanting everyone to know she was up for this more than ever, thumped down on them aggressively. Donna felt the force, but did not react, she just returned to her corner.

"What the fuck was that?" PD asked in an inquisitive high-pitched voice. "I had to stop her talking," was all Donna could say. PD tapped her gloves together, "Well get a grip of yourself, because you need all the nous you can muster right now. Stay calm and do the job you have to do." Then he could not contain himself, "Did you see how she fell? Fucking hilarious." She smiled, he playfully slapped her across the chin. "Focus Donna, no mistakes."

* * *

Ding. Round 1. As she approached the centre of the ring to begin combat, Donna knew she was not fully alert, all these thoughts are getting in my head; how long do I have to make this last and should I make a show of it or lay down straight away. A solid jab on her nose, of both force and venom, interrupted her thoughts. This girl does not know it is a stitch up and if I do not have my wits about me, I could get a hiding for real.

Quickly she was into fight mode and avoided the next slow, predictable jab with ease and ducked under a cross. Latrice knew Donna had felt the force of the jab and her confidence rose. She put together a combination and tried to end the fight, there and then, with an exaggerated hay maker. None connected, not even close. The realisation was starting to dawn; Donna was a class above her. This dampened her confidence, as quickly as it had been lifted. She was getting more and more frustrated as that first punch apart, she was chasing shadows and could not lay a glove on Donna at all.

Donna did not throw too many punches as she concentrated more on keeping out of harm's way; she dummied, shimmied, made out a huge right was on its way and then pulled out of landing it. She let rip with the odd jab and body blow, in an attempt to calm this girl down. Surely she would feel the power, become all too aware of the defensive skills she was up against and back off? Then we can both have a painless night.

The bell rang and she went to touch gloves with her opponent in a show of mutual respect, but it was positively ignored and all she got in return was a stare of utter contempt. She made her way back to her corner where PD was waiting with a stool and sponge. He took the gum shield out and washed it in some fresh-ish water. She rinsed her mouth from a bottle of luke warm water, spat it out in the bucket and sank back against the corner post. PD splashed far too much water in her face from his sponge. "What the fuck...." That boyish grin was there. "Just keeping you awake," he said as he towelled the drips away.

Ding. Round 2. "Stop running bitch and let's have a real fight or are you too scared?" Latrice had to even the field as much as she could and a few more barbs might rattle her opponent. She knew a tear up was far more her style than all this clever shit. "OK then," Donna replied, she dodged the latest attack and lifted Latrice off her feet with an uppercut just below the ribs. Then she stepped back and said, "Every time you open your gob I'm going to hurt you bad," and then did some Ali jigging on the spot. Latrice was hurting for the rest of the round. Whilst she engaged in some light sparring, she did not even try to land any heavy stuff.

Donna knew how easy she was finding this, as she was able to avoid most of the stuff coming her way and could pick off her opponent whenever she liked. She really hoped this girl had finally got it at last and would realise she had no place being in the same ring as her. Even the punches that connected were lacking any power. Donna had moved out of distance for any real danger or just blocked the main force of them by the time they connected. More like it. PD felt happier that her head was clear now, but he knew that at some point she was going to have to get close enough to take a decent punch or this could be the first one nil result in boxing history; one punch to nil!

During the break in rounds, Donna noticed in the other corner that the coach was lashing into Latrice and clearly winding her up. She could not hear what was being said, but by his animated arm actions he was telling her to take Donna out. His displeasure at what he'd seen that round was evident. Time to say good night, Donna prepared herself for this to be the round she took one; anywhere near the head and I will go down like the lights have gone out.

Ding. Round 3. She got off her seat and as they came together Latrice said, "Bitch, you made me look bad and you are going to pay for that. Once YOU have paid, I'm going to slap your kids and anyone else who says they know you just to prove you were in my pocket. Suck on that, bitch."

That bloody coach has done a job on you and now we are back to square one. Mouthing off again and you thinking you can take me out with some huge bomb of yours. Before this ends, you are going to know who the chump is and I will shut that gob of yours.

"Yeah, well look, learn and then stop your whining."

Donna stuck her chin out and then withdrew the whole top half of her body. Latrice took the bait and ended up missing by a mile. "I feel a draft, do you feel a draft?" She goaded and added, "Your coach is not going to like that." Latrice was still smarting from her rollicking. She had to get under Donna's skin. All she could do was hurl more threats and insults to get Donna to come out from behind that defensive shell she was having no impact on. Donna expertly evaded the latest jab and connected with a straight punch to the nose. A trickle of blood immediately gave away the effectiveness of the punch. "Bitch, you are going to pay for that." Instantly Donna connected again, this time with enough force to throw the head back. Blood speckled up in the air and then spotted the canvas. "Keep talking, please keep talking." Latrice knew she was in for a long, painful night. Even her main weapon of goading Donna was back firing. She looked to her corner for advice, support, something. Her trainer was waving a fist at her, clearly mad that she was making him look so bad.

She stepped forward and then back to give her a semblance of distance from Donna, so she could regroup.

I have to stick to what I know and just hope you drop those arms when you get angry.

"Keep looking over your shoulder after tonight, because you and yours are getting messed up." Donna looked at her and her face gave away her amazement of how stupid this whole thing is. It was all bluff, because if only she knew, Latrice was going to win, so any threats were empty beyond belief. The bell went and they both stared hard at each other. PD grabbed her and escorted her back to the corner. "You Ok?" he said, "Still in control or are you letting her get in your head?" She was. How ridiculous is that. "Yeah, a bit. But back on plan now, so stay calm. I will give her one last tap and then lay down." He raised the water bottle, she sipped and spat and then he greased her eyes again. "Good, because if you keep battering her every time she rants, the gulf in ability will be too obvious and the masses will smell a rat. I would rather you do not piss Russ off any more. It ends this round."

Ding Round Four.

No chat from across the ring, that's unexpected and based on the previous three rounds, unusual. OK, I will let her near and let's be done with all this. They jockeyed for position in the centre of the ring and Donna conceded ground as she felt for the ropes on her back. Latrice sensed an opportunity, but rather than try to land her favoured big punch, she edged in until she had Donna penned in.

Latrice's ears were ringing from what her trainer had said, the bombs were not landing, so try to get in some clinches and land a few meaningful blows from there. If all else fails, get close and rough this girl up. Donna pushed her back into the ropes to allow her adversary to follow in, this will work fine as it is not easy to see how good a punch is in a clinch. She felt a short punch to her side, which did not trouble her, but she acted a little hurt. Latrice saw the reaction and immediately let go with a stray elbow and was pleased to feel it connect with Donna's temple. The ref pulled Latrice off and waved a finger at her. He checked with Donna that she was OK and issued the signal for the bout to continue. Latrice's trainer was in full flow now, cheering his fighter like she had won the whole match. You dirty cow, you will rue that! We had got so close to ending this too.

She pushed herself off the ropes and eyeballed her adversary with eyes that burned a little more into Latrice than previously.

Enough of this bollocks. A little more pain for you and then I will play dead.

She moved back into position with sublime boxing artistry. Almost effortlessly she regained the centre of the ring with nothing more than a dummy, a side step and a pretend haymaker, that never grew beyond being half grown. Right then, time for one more lesson and then let's get out of here.

Donna threw her weight from her left to her right foot and then back again quickly, so it was unclear which direction she was going. As soon as she saw Latrice was off balance, she let go with a half decent left cross that was meant to end any pretence, once and for all, this moron had of thinking she had a chance of winning for real.
I will teach her who the boss is and then do what is expected of me. She knew by experience when a punch lands flush, and this one had landed very sweetly. Too sweetly. Latrice went down with her eyes rolling before she hit the canvas. The referee saw her head bounce and knew she was out cold. He was instantly waving his hands and frantically prising her gum shield out.

No way, was all Donna could hear blaring in her head. For the first time ever, with any opponent, she was half hoping this stupid, mouthy cow would get up off the canvas. From the limp body and sea of people who had appeared from nowhere to help, that was simply not going to happen. Perhaps, the earlier blows had softened her up, perhaps she had let the mouthing and the elbow get to her too much and added more power than she had meant to and perhaps this girl just could not take any sort of semi-tidy punch. Who cares? It did not matter, because the whole illusion was blown right out of the water. Donna was unable to move, seemingly frozen to the spot.

Russ was not watching too intently, because he knew the result, so all this playing at boxing was of little interest. However, Donna's game changer of a punch had got his attention and then some. It was like time stopped, gradually accelerated into slow motion, before arriving at normal speed. Within seconds, Russ was consumed by a temper that was at warp speed.

PD was quickly by her side and put Donna in a protective one-armed bear hug as he shepherded her back to the corner. "Are you crazy or stupid or both," he mumbled as he pushed through the crowd in the ring. Whilst it may have seemed he was shouting at any random person, Donna knew it was aimed at her. All the time Donna was transfixed by the sight of the girl on the floor as she had laid quite a few people out, but none had been so out of it as this. She felt physically sick. Through years of experience PD knew what to expect; he jabbed the side of the bucket into her arm, so she knew where to puke.

She did not know who did what, but all of a sudden the limp body jerked a bit and life slowly flowed back into the girl. The medical people started to ask Latrice basic questions but in loud voices to be heard above the din; *What is your name? Where are you?*

A small torch was shone into her eyes; she looked away, blinked wildly and shook her head. Two of the men surrounding her placed an arm under each armpit and lifted her up, semi dragging her to the corner where she was placed on her stool. Latrice was showing signs of becoming more aware of her surroundings and any sick bastards who might hope she would not make it, seemed to be heading for disappointment. As she regained more of her senses and then began answering more of the basic questions she was being asked, a huge wave of relief surged through Donna. The mental relief caused a physical reaction as she grabbed the bucket and produced a horrible, smelly mouthful of bile, retching and heaving. She wiped her mouth and could feel her body shaking as if she was in freezing waters. In fact, she knew she was still quite warm from the exertions of the fight; if you could call it that.

PD slapped her across the face with just enough force to get her attention. "You listening to me? God knows what sort of a fireball of fury you have just set off in one of the nastiest pieces of work this neighbourhood knows, but we have got to start thinking RIGHT NOW about what we are going to do." His voice was shaky, but full of urgency and she knew he was scared. PD had done the trick and she returned in mind and body to what was happening.

"What do you mean 'we'? You keep the fuck out of this old man. I hit her and I will deal with it." He stopped messing with her gloves, grabbed her wrists tightly and looked her full in the eyes. His eyes had been excited as they darted all over the place, but now they were fixed on hers with a stare she had not seen before and would not want to again. "Words like that hurt me more than any man's punch ever has. Whatever shit you are in I will be there with you and if you ever doubt that or try to say we are not then................" That's as far as he got, before he looked down and began roughly wrestling her gloves off. Yanking at the laces and ripping at the tape. "PD, I'm sorry."

He was right, what was she going to do? She looked over at Russ's table and he was clearly getting agitated; frowning, biting his lip and jabbing his finger towards the ring. It would not have been about the money as he did not have a need for the pocket change this would give him. It was all about the reputation and she knew her actions had seemed to make a fool out of him. Russ suddenly flew off his chair. Before it flew backwards and hit the floor, he was moving towards the ring. She had no idea why, but something was impelling Donna to get on her feet. With everyone looking, Russ dodged through the ropes and headed towards her.

"You stupid little cow. Quite what the fuck you think you were doing I will never know, but you will pay big time for taking the piss out of me......" He was somehow restraining himself from physically laying into her, as there were a lot of witnesses and she was a girl, but those voices holding him back were losing the battle in his head.

He lifted a fist that had her name all over it, but before it could land, Rich was in his way. Russ thought Rich was being the dutiful son and making sure he did not do anything in public he shouldn't. "It's alright son, I can wait to deal with her. You lady, will not think this was quite such a clever thing to do once I have finished with you and anyone connected to you. PD, you make sure she doesn't think about leaving town or I will give you what she had coming." PD was about to make things 100 times worse, when Rich spoke up. He was firm enough to get his dad's attention, but did so at a volume which would not generate interest from anyone else.

"Dad, you need to calm down or it will be obvious what was going on here tonight." Russ felt the fog of fury slowly lift as he heard what his son was saying, and he stopped pointing at Donna. He clapped his hands over his head as if congratulating her. It could not have looked any more awkward.

"You are right Rich, thank you. PD, get her out back now and then we'll see how fucking smart she thinks she is." Rich kept his voice soft and low, but with as much intensity as he could muster he said,
"What are you going to do?"
"I'm going to squeeze her neck until I feel she understands why trying to fuck me over is a bad idea. If she's lucky enough to survive that, she can tell me how she plans to repay me for this balls up."
"Dad, I don't want you to that. Let's go out back and think this through calmly."
"I will be calm. She's the one who might get a bit stirred up."
"I can't let you touch her."
"Relax, you big Jessie. I promise I'll try not to kill her."

"No dad, you're not getting it. We've been seeing each other for a while and I love her." Rich glanced at Donna, but neither showed any emotion. They both focused back on Russ, sensing the volcano that was bubbling up and would soon be erupting. "If you want to hurt her you are going to have to do it through me."

Russ heard the words and then time seemed to stop for him again. His features were still and he seemed to be looking through his son as he took in what was being said. Then remarkedly calmly, he said, "We are not doing this in public. You, and her, get to the dressing room. Dean, get Chan and meet us out back and clear the fucking room." With that he exited the ring and barged his way through those who had wanted a front row seat for what had turned out to be the main event of the evening. They moved out of his way as best they could and made sure no eye contact was made. Some were too hemmed in or just too slow and Russ went around, over or through anyone in his way. It was reminiscent of the running of the bulls in Spain, as the people who wanted to get close to the action, could not move for the throng of the crowd if the Bulls suddenly turned their way.

As she thumped back down on the stool, PD knew he needed to calm Donna down or who knows what might happen. He leaned forward and whispered in her ear, holding her head to make sure she heard him. "The warm down might have to wait." His cheeky old grin was back and she knew he was trying to help. She also knew this was his nerves helping him deal with the worry of what might happen next.

Donna looked at Rich.
"Now you've done it."
"Me? I have done it! Unbelievable. That mound of jelly sat on that stool is all your work. Now do yourself and all of us a favour and try to keep your brain engaged for the next little while and hope we can find a way out of this that doesn't involve any unpleasantness. Although, I can't even convince myself of that just now."

Considering it was one of her easiest fights ever, it was ridiculous how weary she felt as she dragged herself off her stool. As she did the attention was even more on her. Some people openly stared at her, whilst others half looked. It was not hard to spot those who had not 'earned' their promised reward and despite clearly being able to afford to lose a few quid, they had a snarl on their face as if she had taken the food off their children's table. Based on what had just happened in the ring, a few were starting to realise the truth, but so what. Making a complaint to Russ about his unsportingness was a no brainer. A few beers would be raised tonight, paid for out of their winnings, to toast Russ getting 'his'. Even some of those who had been tipped off how to bet would not be unhappy to see Russ be made a fool. On reflection they would see those losses as money well spent for that much amusement.

As she dipped through the ropes some halfwits made a few choice comments, but she had been called a bitch and whore many times and the lack of originality never ceased to amaze her. Normally she would not be averse to staring these idiots out, but she kept her head down as she followed PD through the melee. She had enough to deal with without taking all this lot on. Her mind was going crazy trying to think what would happen next. It seemed a longer walk back than it had coming out as she was pushed, nudged and barracked all the way. She felt Rich behind her and between PD leading, and him bringing up the rear, no-one landed anything physically painful on her.

Russ was staring at the wall away from Donna as PD moved aside once they were in the room. She felt Rich beside her and he put a protective arm around her waist and gave a little squeeze. She looked up at him and saw how scared he was. His face was white, and he was staring firmly at the back of his dad's head. Waiting, just waiting to see where this was going. "PD, get out. I do not need you to stay. This is family business," Russ kept his voice controlled, but it had a certain menace about it. "She's family to me," PD said and sat down to signal, end of discussion. "If you stay you are involved full on, no half measures - understand?" PD shrugged and nodded, which he realised merged into one clumsy movement, so he leaned fully back in the chair and hoped no-one had noticed.

"Right, who the fuck wants to tell me what is going on here? Dean; you in on this?"
"Me? No! I guessed tonight and that's the first I had known of it."
"Then you are as stupid in the head as he is in the pants." That made no sense, but none of them felt like pointing that out at this precise moment.

Dean looked scolded and gave Rich a cold stare; here I am getting grief off the old man when I have done absolutely nothing wrong. "Dad.......," before he'd got any further Russ had swivelled round and a huge fist connected with Rich in the pit of his stomach. He collapsed to the floor gasping for breath and groaning through pain and shock. It had happened so quickly he had no time to brace himself. Chan moved in and placed his hand across his boss's chest as he knew two things; if he did not stop Russ then he would really go to town on his son and secondly, he would regret that for a long time. Russ felt the shovel of a hand firmly restraining him and looked up at Chan. The sensation in his cheeks and forehead was feverish and he realised his whole face was on fire with anger. He grasped what his hired muscle was doing and roughly pushed the arm away before moving himself a few steps back.

He waved his finger inches from her face. "See what you have done you stupid little cow, you have come between me and my boy and for that you will pay big time." He was used to the merest flare of his temper turning everyone submissive and compliant, but he knew that was not going to happen today. He wanted to think and staring at Donna was not helping with that. He turned and stepped into a space away from her. Impulse placed his hand over his face, as if to block it all out. He slowly moved it all the way down, until it was cradling his chin. He had got his thoughts together. "Here's what will happen........"

Rich interrupted him, his voice full of disgust, pain and mostly plain rebellion,

"I will tell YOU what will happen DAD." He reached for a chair to hoist himself up, still holding his guts with one arm to soothe the excruciating pain in his abdomen. "I'm going to take my GIRLFRIEND away from here right now. If you ever want to see me again you will 'deal' with the prats who lost their money tonight. Then tomorrow, I will bring Donna to see you and we will sort this out, but you be sure of one thing; she is not going away, because I can't live without her. You had better come to terms with that. By the way; decent punch even if it was sly." He patted his stomach lightly and said, "Never, do that again."

Russ felt the fury rising again and moved menacingly towards Rich, when someone spoke from the open doorway, where they had clearly heard everything that had been said. "I think I should come to lunch too...don't you, Russ?" Donna looked at the man, spun her head to Rich, then at Russ and back at the man again.

"Dad................." He put up his index finger to stop her saying anything else.
"Just thought I would sneak in and see my little girl fight. Then, all this kicks off." He locked his laser eyes on Russ.
"You probably know you have two choices, but I will spell them out for you anyway. Leave her alone or kill me. Good luck with that, because others have tried and as you can see, I'm still around." The stare-out lasted for what seemed like ages, before Dog grinned and said calmly, "You ready Donna?" He moved his eyes from Russ to Dean, who was wondering what was happening, and on to the hired help. He nodded in his direction, "Chan." His nod was reciprocated, and he left, taking Donna with him. As she was holding tightly on to Rich, he joined them.

CHAPTER 19.

"This life of ours, this is a wonderful life. If you can get through life like this and get away with it, hey, that's great. But it's very, very unpredictable. There's so many ways you can screw it up."- Paul Castellano.

Russ fronted up Chan. "Ahhh, that was a nice moment. Shouldn't you have done something? I mean I thought I paid you to avoid situations like that and you did nothing. For fucks sake, what is going on here tonight - go give him a hiding and drag Rich back." Chan was fed up of all this shit that kept coming his way of late. He needed to regain control, because he had taken more than enough of people not treating him well. "You sure, you want me to do that?" Chan said in a calm way. "Now you are doing my thinking for me are you? Why wouldn't I want what I have just asked for?" Dean was still in the room, but Russ did not care about that as he questioned Chan.

"Because, if I had not stopped you earlier your relationship with your son might not have recovered and if I do what you tell me to now, that could create the same outcome. Did you know she was Dog's daughter? We both know that he will threaten your family if you threaten his. Whilst I can do so much to protect you, I can't be with you all, every hour of the day."

Dean saw a chance to impress his dad and who knows to make things better, so he jumped up. "I will go get Rich dad and heaven help that nutter if he gets in my way." He was stopped in his tracks by Russ, who pushed a big hand into his chest that forced him to sit down again.

"Chan, on a scale of 1 to 10, what chance would you give Dean against Dog?"
"Big fat zero." Chan delivered his line without emotion. Russ was gaining some control of his thoughts again.
"Thank you Dean, but I know of Dog and to be honest Chan would not find him a walkover, so no thinking because he's an old 'un he'll be easy. He won't. OK Chan, you have never seen me wrong before and cowardice is not something you are strong on, but you tell me now if I need that bastard sorting real good, you are my man."
"Boss, I am. But we need to really think this through and if you do not mind me saying, not tonight. If your judgement isn't clouded, then you are not human. Rich is involved, a girl he really likes is involved and dealing with Dog is not like giving a

poor payer a scare. He will keep coming back until he is stopped for good and that could have serious issues for happy families."

Dean felt confused. By stopping him going after this man, had his dad protected or belittled him? Whoever this Dog was, he could not remember Russ or Chan acting this way about anyone else. He looked at his dad,

"You know this Dog person then?"
"More like know of, and I guess the same for Chan. He's been locked away a few times for hurting people bad and Dog, is short for Wild Dog, because he doesn't stop until he's pulled off whoever he happens to be kicking the shit out of. Whoever is stupid enough to pull him off is likely to get theirs next. He's mellowed of late, so I heard, but of course you and cock brain did not do your homework before choosing this Donna. Now I'm in a position where I may have to put this dog down. Go home. I will think what we do tomorrow, because tonight I need another stiff drink and that's all. Dean, I need to know everyone, who is anyone, who lost money here tonight. We may have some kissing and making up to do after this shit storm."

"Do we need to keep Stoney sweet anymore?" Dean asked almost in passing. "Can't see why, that lucky bastard probably made a killing here tonight, so he won't be a worry. Why do you ask?" "His missus is an incredible shag and I was just checking how long I would be her plumber of choice." Russ eyed Dean with no shortage of silly macho pride that he should have been over years ago. With all this going on his main concern is getting his end away. "You check her pipes out one more time and then be done with it; OK? Best we do not upset anyone else eh....... go on, piss off. You too Chan."

They left quickly, Chan manhandling Dean out of the room before he said anything else. A few minutes alone time was well needed by Russ, before he made his way home. Then his honed senses rang an alarm in his head. He wasn't on his own. His head was facing the door, but he was talking into the shadows of the room.

"Well PD, my old mucker, we have got ourselves a belting little conundrum here, haven't we?" PD sat forward, "I thought you'd forgotten I was here." He guessed Russ would be looking at him, so to avoid that mini eye to eye battle, he looked at his trainers. "You should be so fucking lucky. I had, but then my radar kicked in and there you are, skulking in the corner trying to blend into the background, like some scared little girl." PD continued looking at his trainers, as if all the answers were in them.

"This is not the time for petty insults, it's just you and me, so let's chat like the two old gits we are, who have known each other for a long time. You are a winner Russ, always have been. When you look like losing you cheat or steal to make sure you win. It's done you very well; money is no longer a problem and never will be, as long as your accountant can keep those tax boys away from you. But this, this is no competition. This could hurt you in ways other than financial. Admit it, if you lost contact with Rich over this you'd be crucified, so you might need to compromise for once in your life. That girl is like my own daughter and, like Dog, I won't stand by if she's hurting. We went along with this stupid game of your boys and hoped it would then go away, that you'd go away. However, a mouthy opponent, unworthy of being in the same ring, Donna not knowing her own ability and here we are. Chan will hurt me if you ask him to, but he won't want to - you know that. Do that too many times and your number one employee could find similar work elsewhere. I know people do not talk to you like this, but it's about time someone other than a 'yes man' had your ear."

Russ loved PD, always had. He had liked being part of his gym when he was much younger, and the affection had remained ever since, but there was a line. "Enough PD. Any more and you will be out of the gym business permanently. You know how these things work. I have lost money and I have lost face here tonight, so no getting too gushy with me. I have to put things right." PD, heaved his body off the chair and headed for the door, talking as he shuffled. "I'm not sure how much of what I said you heard, judging by what you just said. So, hear this. I have no family, but I'm hurting for Donna. I can't begin to imagine what this is like for you, with your own blood involved. However, on top of the money and the 'face', do not risk losing your son. It cannot be worth it, I mean, over a chicken feed fight. Night Russ. Somehow I think we'll be in touch soon."

CHAPTER 20.

"All I know is that you are the nicest thing I have ever seen, I wish we could see if we could be something..." - Kate Nash.

Dog fetched them to this spit and sawdust pub, The Peacock, where he was ordering the drinks and chatting away to the barmaid like nothing had happened. On the way Donna had explained about her and Rich. Dog had taken it fairly well. "There I am, planning to kick the shit out of you and now we're on the same side. Good job I found out before I came visiting."

Donna looked at Rich across the table and in her best childlike, mocking tone said,
"How's your belly? Did dad-da hurt his little soldier?"
"He caught me unaware, you inconsiderate cow." She could not contain her wicked smile and even through his pain and dented pride he could see the funny side.
"When you said, 'You will have to go through me', I was hoping for a bit more protection, or is laying down on the floor groaning what I can expect from you whenever a bit of bother comes our way?"
"You are so funny, I'm not sure what hurts more, his punch or your jokes."

Thank heavens PD was OK. On the way Donna had realised he was not with them, but a quick phone call put her mind at rest. He mumbled something about 'a few words with Russ', but he was on his way home. If nothing else, the relief she felt was freeing up her mind to mess Rich about. She was sure Russ had done his thing, but PD was not sounding shaken or anything. He even did his Uncle Albert impression, from *Only Fools & Horses*, saying that Russ could not scare someone who had taken on the whole German fleet singlehandedly. That rubbish impression had reassured her he was definitely OK. Whatever relief or playfulness she felt right now was not going to last. She knew this was not over for any of them.

Her old man joined them and placed their drinks on the table; two lagers, a still water and three vodka shots. Fighter or not, a bit of alcohol would do Donna some good and if she refused, he could make use of it. Rich immediately went for the short, he knew he could not stop shaking and he hoped the alcohol would pacify whatever else was going on in his body. He necked it in one. After a couple of seconds, he shook his head to quell the liquid explosion as it did its work. Donna looked at her dad, shrugged and then together they downed theirs in one too. Dog tried his best to mask the pleasure pain, but could not prevent the giveaway sign of his lips pulling completely back to reveal his teeth as the sting kicked in. Donna screwed her eyes and nose up as tightly as it was possible to. As the aftermath descended, her pupils dilated and she made an O shape with her mouth. A quick shake of the head and she was compos mentis again.

"So, what happens now?" Rich asked.
"That depends on your dad," Dog said. "Hopefully, he will calm down, make peace with his 'buddies' who lost money on the night, see that blood is thicker than water and want to keep you close and get to know Donna better." Donna slowly turned to Rich, who was mirroring her open mouth, incredulous look.
"Or," he continued, "his rather well known temper, and massive ego, will override any feelings he has for you. Then he will come after all of us, with the intention of getting you back in line and me, and her, probably dead, or at least hospitalised for a while. All of which he could argue we had coming. What we've got to make sure of is he doesn't get anywhere near them kids."

"I'm off to the lav," Rich got up and headed off.
"You ok dad?" He glanced at her with an 'are you for real?' type look and then stared deep into his pint.
"Suppose it's at times like this you wish you'd had boys rather than us girls."
"Nope," he said emphatically,
"All I wanted was kids I could be very proud of," and with that he looked up and his whole face creased into a warm grin.
"Oh dad, thank you," she got up and put her arms around his neck and squeezed him tight.
"Who knows, I still might have time to produce one that can do that......" She let go and slapped him hard on the back of his shoulder. Then she sat down. It had been a horrible few months and it was not finished yet, but she had never felt closer to her dad. Rich appeared again and in her head all she could hear was,
'With what I have got coming could I have landed myself with a bigger couple of twats to see me through this?' She could not contain her grin and they both looked at her, "What???"

CHAPTER 21.

"You can go a long way with a smile. You can go a lot farther with a smile and a gun."
—Al Capone.

Donna was determined to keep things as normal as possible, so she went to the gym for a workout. It was modest by her normal standards, to say the least, but she felt good to be getting rid of some pent-up energy and was pleased to catch up with PD. He was in his normal playful mode.

"I hear they're knocking some flats down around the corner soon. I know, why not offer to do it for them with your big punch," she took line after line of the same.
"If you do not shut up, I will mistake you for a block of flats."
"Yes Donna, no Donna, please don't hit me Donna. You are just so unaware of how strong you are." He adopted a shaky, pleading voice and cowered behind his hands that were raised in mock protection.

"I take it no contact from Tomkins Ltd yet?" Time for him to get serious.
"Nah, the fucker is making me wait."
"He will, and obviously I don't need to tell such a laid back and responsible person as you this," he coughed a little and raised his eyebrows at her before continuing, safe in the knowledge his point had been made, "but, when he does you need to play things very cool. We are all in deep shit over this, so think first lady. I'm of little consequence, and for that matter neither are your dad or Rich, but those kids are! They need YOU to steer them through the next few years of their life. Have them at the front of your brain as you begin speaking please." He turned and began walking away.

"Hey, old man, had you thought about getting some new trainers?" He glanced down at his footwear, then at her.
"Why? What's wrong with these beauties?" He had bought them in a sale a couple of years back and they might not be pristine, but he was not going to waste money replacing them until they were falling apart.
"Just making sure you will be able to run when Chan is sent after you?" Gallows humour.
"Huh, he doesn't frighten me with his huge bulk, massive strength and advanced fighting skills. Take more than that to frighten me.................. where did you say I

could get some new spikes from?" He was moving off and waving a finger of admonishment at her above his head.

* * *

There was a firm knock on the door and Sam had one foot on the floor as he instinctively, typical boy like, made a move to see who was there. "Do not even think about it Sam," Donna bellowed through from another room. How could she see me, he wondered and assumed his previous position?

It was Chan.
"Come to beat me up have you?" She sneered.
"Of course." Chan did not change his expression at all as he delivered his dry response. "Mr. Tomkins would like to see you tomorrow, in his office." She cocked her head to one side and was about to say, 'Oh he would, would he', but only got as far as, 'Oh he....', when Chan raised a massive hand that acted as a stop sign. "Let's not be silly. You will be seeing Mr. Tomkins, in his office, tomorrow, at 3pm; that is clear and beyond doubt. If you are meant to be working, call in sick. Get someone to look after the kids and for whatever other million reasons that are ringing through your head that need sorting, then....... sort them." He kept the same well practiced expression that he knew gave nothing away. He was sure he could not have been clearer, however he decided to emphasise his point.

"Have I kicked your door in?"
"No."
"Have I picked you up off the floor by your throat and carried you all the way to Mr. Tomkins office like that?"
"No!"
"Then be where you should be at 3pm or I will do both things. To be honest I would rather not, because it will cost you a new door, I do not like having to rough women up and you are speaking to him anyhow. One more point that Mr. Tomkins was emphatic about. Do not tell Rich or your dad. If you tell them, you could put them in danger. Just come on your own."
"Beneath all that front, are you a nice bloke really Chan?"
"Rav said to ask you a similar question." He half nodded, half smirked, stepped back and as he moved off, daylight flooded back in through the door.
"3pm. Be there," he left a parting shot in a loudish voice over his shoulder.

She shut the door and felt instantly sick. It was obvious Russ was going to make contact, so she knew it was going to happen, but up to now there was always a chance he might not. She had used that fanciful possibility to block out the reality.

However, now it had moved from possible to actual, her mind kicked in and hope was replaced by fear running wild. She wanted to talk to Rich, but how could she? She doubted Russ would really do damage to his son, but what about if he did and it was not a bluff? She could not risk that, so she had no-one to talk to and the dread of doing this alone was feeding her terror. She was a novice in this world she had got sucked into and Russ was the master of dark arts such as these. If she did tell Rich and he confronted his dad, with, or more likely without her agreement, then who knows what might happen to her and the kids. Rich stays unaware of the meeting.

What about dad? She was far less worried about his physical wellbeing as she knew everyone, including the mighty Chan, would seriously have to think twice before taking him on. Still, there was the nagging doubt of what might happen if she reneged on what she had been told. No point being prissy about whether she had agreed or not, as Russ was probably not the sort of person to let that stop him decreeing a hiding. She would have felt much better about the meeting if she could just talk to someone, but it was not a gamble worth taking.

She checked on Maggie and Sam. "Can you go to Aunty Layla's please? Tell her I have a couple of bits to do and I'll call for you in a while." She switched the TV off, which always did the trick to get them moving. They scuttled off.

Donna could feel how the endless variety of visions that were flooding her head, were taking over her ability to think and draining her already low reservoirs of will and resilience. She had visions of Rich being in the office when she got there beaten to a pulp, covered in blood, lying limp on the floor; or Layla, what about Layla? It was nothing to do with her at all, but that did not mean she would not get sucked in if it meant Donna would get hurt. She went to even deeper and darker places we only go when extreme circumstances open those bolted doors. What about if he killed someone as a lesson to her and to show his cohorts he was still 'the man?' Her dad or one of the kids?

She thumped her head with the heel of her hand to make these images go away and then broke out into an uncontrollable sob. Her body was shaking and her shoulders heaved up and down as she fought to reign in her emotions; she lost the battle. The outpouring of emotions lasted probably a minute or so, although it felt so much longer. It had been building up and even though it felt horrible, it was probably a good thing to let loose with a few tears and purge some of the crap she had been carrying with them. As she regained a semblance of control over herself, she sniffed at the snot and wiped this and the tears away with her sleeve.

She slowly got up and all the other images were made small, insignificant and black & white, as a picture of Helen radiated at her in full, glorious colour. She kept it on the side near the front door, so she could say hello and goodbye to her sister whenever she entered or left the flat. She began to regain power over her faculties and grabbed a tissue with which she dabbed at her eyes and blew her nose. She breathed in, held it, and then out again very deeply.

She could not let anyone even suspect what was going on, so she steeled herself for the rest of the day. She would need to put on the acting performance of her life. Then tomorrow, she would attend this 'meeting' and see what that mean, ugly bastard wanted. She resolved to pay the piper, if she could. Another deep filling of the lungs and powerful expelling of the air and the haze was clearing. She promised herself one thing; she would attend as the Donna she saw herself to be and would hold her head high. The outcome was cast already, quite probably, so no point in trying to be something she was not. That lifted her spirits and she picked up a child's trainer from the floor and headed for the kitchen to start preparing the evening meal.

Her mobile chirped, it was Rich. She pressed the button to decline the call and stop the ringing. She might not be telling him everything, but at least if she did not speak to him she would not be lying.

CHAPTER 22.

True courage is being afraid, and going ahead and doing your job anyhow, that's what courage is. - Norman Schwarzkopf.

Layla would look after the kids and Donna had swapped shifts at work, so the practicalities were all taken care of. Still torn about telling dad and Rich, she decided to play things as she was instructed, although she had contacted PD and made him aware where she was going and that she would call him once the meeting was over. If it got beyond 6pm and he hadn't heard then he could tell whoever he liked, because she was going to be in need of help at that point. Assuming it was not too late! She was scared, no point flowering it up, this was serious shit. Talk about walking into the Lion's Den. Her stomach was going over and over, but she was determined of one thing; this useless great bully was not going to make her cry. She was early, but so what, get in there and let's deal with whatever is coming.

She saw a pleasant looking girl on reception; "My name is Donna and I'm here to see Mr. Tomkins." The girl glanced at a sheet on her desk, "Please take a seat." She lifted the phone, "Your appointment is here....... Donna." She held the phone away from her head as he had obviously, curtly, slammed the phone down. "He shouldn't be long," and offered a smile that lacked any sincerity.

Ten minutes later a cross looking man, dressed in a suit and tie, but with a nose and face that had been punched far too many times over many years, came out. I hope he hasn't upset him before I have to go in was ringing in her head. She had not heard any raised voices so either the man always looked angry or the room was sound proofed.

Oh shit, the room could be sound proofed!

She began seeing all sorts of torture equipment laid out in her mind and thought about legging it when the phone rang, and she was told to;

"Go through please, that door, turn right and the door nearly opposite should be open."

As she entered, Russ was sat, facing the window with his steeple fingers firmly in place and did not immediately turn around. Yet more intimidation tactics, she thought, and began looking around for anything torture like. It was a big room for an office, but not very full of 'stuff' and aside for a letter opener, she could not see anything remotely built to cause human pain. Oh, except for Chan, who was quietly lurking near the door. She let out a short gasp as her eyes feasted on him and was annoyed that she kept doing that. Then she nodded at him, in a way acquaintances do, and felt a little embarrassed when he did not nod back. This was not her at all and she had to get control of herself, so she did a very mature thing. She pulled an 'I don't care' face at Chan, accompanied by sticking her tongue out. That felt better, much more like her; stop grinning, he's turning.

The expensive swivel chair did not make a sound as it effortlessly swung him to face her. She did not feel quite so clever again all of a sudden. Fingers in their normal position, he was staring at her, clearly all part of a well-practiced tool of intimidation.

What do I do? Stare him out and risk naffing him off even more or look away and look weak.

Thankfully he brought her train of thought to a close. "Got ourselves into a bit of a situation, haven't we?" He stopped speaking and she wondered if it was a question or not. "Normally, you have a lot to say for yourself, from the little I have seen of you, so please don't be coy today. Tell me what's going through that head of yours right now, that might make me feel better and before hell on earth rains down on you and yours."

Her throat was dry. She had a choice; she could act out being someone she clearly was not, or, be her and take the consequences. She swallowed, here goes, "Right now, I am shitting bricks, but I'm sure you already knew that. You've 'invited' me here as I have upset you badly with Mount Everest blocking my escape route and I'm sure a few people have encountered some 'grief' in this room. I am extremely frightened of what could happen to me and the people I love. Now, do you want me to plead for my life and beg forgiveness like some useless twat or can we speak freely?" Inwardly he smiled to himself, just when you think you have seen it all the biggest pair of balls ever to stand in front of him belonged to a girl. "Please continue, I mean you are practically family, aren't you? Chan, try to look less evil will you? It's scaring poor Donna." Chan muttered "Yes boss," and carried on looking and acting exactly as he had been.

"This might be a normal day's work for you and I'm sure it's all some massive joke, but it's not normal to me. I haven't been close to my dad for a long time, but he's still my dad and I do not want any harm coming to him. Maggie and Sam may not be mine, but I love them with all my heart and will do anything, ANYTHING, to protect them. My friend Layla didn't deserve to be involved, but apparently is, purely because we are friends. Like so much of this shit that isn't fair. Then there's Rich. I really care about him and who knows one day it could turn into love and everything that goes with that. You started off by saying 'we've got ourselves into a bit of a situation', but from where I'm standing there's little of the 'we've' about it. I was targeted by your boys, for some stupid reason, and then they put me in with a mouth on legs who had a glass chin and somehow this has all become my fault in your eyes.

As for what to do about where we've landed up, it's all very new to me so I'm guessing all walking away with no hard feelings is not on the cards." She inquisitively raised her eyebrows at Russ. He did not even twitch a muscle. "Thought not. Money wise you have made it clear that what happened is of no consequence, but I do understand what I have done and why you have gone off on one. I want to resolve this, I really do, but I need to know what it is I can do."

Russ hadn't stopped looking at Donna, in fact he hadn't blinked. Still he stared through her. Eventually, he turned to face Chan and then slowly, very slowly, he faced Donna again. "You are one piece of work and you are getting better and better at these little speeches you keep making." The adrenaline made Donna want to speak, but she saw Russ hold up a hand and with no lack of irritation he looked at his desk. She knew what this meant and stopped herself. She was staring at the top of his head, his hand still raised and he was not moving. She glanced at Chan, but he was looking straight ahead, appearing oblivious to what his boss was doing. He's probably seen him act way weirder than this she thought. Naughty schoolgirl like, she waited for the 'headmaster' to regain his composure.

"As I was saying." He immediately paused to show he was in control. "Your 'speech' suggests you think this can be resolved and that somehow you have the power to do something. First of all, that's presumptive on your part. Secondly, you have no power. Whether you live or die is in my gift." He paused again as he needed time for that to sink in, would it soften her at all? Visibly, it hadn't.

That's interesting, I have seen very hard men melt after one of my 'live or die' show stopper statements, but not this girl. OK, let's take it up a notch.

"I have a solution. Someone you love gets hurt. You pick. In my business, which you admit you do not understand, I have to keep order or else people will see weakness. That invites trouble. You wanted to know, now you do."

She looked at him with a hate he was accustomed to being on the end of. He just gave her a false grin and a shrug of his shoulders. In a low voice she said, "How about your son?" Shit, there was her anger taking over again and she knew it was a mistake as she was saying it. He knew too and milked it. "I thought you said it could grow into 'love'. I wonder what Rich will say when he knows you'd sacrifice him above all the others; not a great way to start a relationship." He looked extremely pleased with himself. "Thank you for that." She knew he was well aware she meant Dean, but to carry on this petty line of conversation was pointless; fifteen love, Mr. Tomkins.

"Now go away and let me know who you choose." He broke his gaze from her and checked his phone, void of any emotion. She felt a strong grip on her upper arm and realised it was Chan leading her out. The meeting was over. She tried to resist and dug her feet in, but it was useless against the might of just the one arm he was using. She began to call out at Russ, "What the..........," but Chan said, "No!" in a way that would stop a Tiger dead in its tracks. He led her out of the room, through the reception area and out into the daylight where he let go of her.

"Nothing silly. Think now," he said. He had done this same routine many times. The overwhelming reaction of people who had been in a similar clash with Russ, was to get back in there and either continue the conversation or land one on him. However, Chan's few words, and his dimensions standing in between them and what they wanted, meant they had to walk away. There was no way of reasoning with Chan that would get him to stand aside, as he was doing the job he was paid for. To consider going around him meant pain and disappointment.

She began to make her way home, but could not resist one last swipe if for nothing else to make her feel better. "Big man eh. Big Chan. My old fellah is going to hear about this and then we will see who needs to think. Have you met him?" She said this with an air of disdain hoping to get a reaction from him, it was done without real thought. What was he going to do? Beg her to call her dad off and rush her back in to see Russ? Chan was standing in his familiar doorman pose looking at her. Many men he had helped leave these meetings left without a word, beaten, down trodden, broken of spirit, but not this one. She had some inner reserves of a kind that was rare.

"Yes, we've met." She felt an uncomfortable flinch as she noticed something in his eyes. Fear? Anger? He never seemed to say more than the minimum, but she was not letting this go. "How did that go for you?" Come on, give me something Chan, the mention of Dog surely had to irk him a little. He paused and considered his words. "It was business, I guess. He felt the need to come tooled up. Why not ask him about it?" She wanted to know more, but he put an end to this particular exchange by saying, "Mr. Tomkins will not wait forever for your answer and then he chooses for himself, before asking you to name the next one and so on and so on. 24 hours or there will be consequences." Did he know how to have the last word or what?

He played these encounters so deadpan and had perfected it over many years. He knew how not to be overtly threatening or menacing, but with an underlying tone of threat and menace. He despatched his message in a matter of fact way and made it quite clear that you comply or pay the price for crossing the boss. She began to turn as if to walk away and then paused mid step.

If I leave now, like this, I will be the same as all the other suckers Russ has bullied, manipulated and squeezed. I am not having that. He has the upper hand for sure with his latest demand, but he does not own me, and I'm buggered if I am going to let them think my spirit has been extinguished.

She turned around, went straight up to Chan and beckoned him to lean forward, "Surely you are not frightened by a girl like me? I just want to whisper something to you." He looked puzzled but replied. "Show me your hands?" She held them out palm up. "Just checking for a duster or anything sharp," he said, then he slowly leaned in. She kissed his cheek and whispered, "I hope daddy didn't scare you too much." She stepped away and began to walk backwards, watching, to see his reaction, before half turning into her normal stride. Chan was flummoxed, this girl is full of surprises. He knew she was saying she was not beaten yet. He released the merest of grins. Donna gave the cheekiest of smiles over her shoulder and headed off.

Once out of sight, the forced smile transformed into a genuine frown. What could be done to stop this situation escalating any further. Come on Donna, think straight. He had thrown a real curve ball in by asking her who was to get the free hospital pass after a visit from Chan or some other heavies. Why had he done this? Surely just for a bit of payback on her as he twisted the knife. He did not like losing that was for sure.

CHAPTER 23.

Some men see things as they are, and ask why. I dream of things that never were, and ask why not. - Robert Kennedy.

Dean rang Rich early in the morning to say, *Do not come into work or pay a visit to Russ,* with or without Donna. The old man needed some thinking time and in the cold light of day a bit of distance for both of them would be no bad thing. Rich knew the danger of this, as it meant Russ would be thinking of how to deal with their situation and if Rich did not strike whilst the iron was hot, he could lose the initiative. However, the problem with going against a direct instruction from Russ, and in doing so rattle him even more, was that he could be outside of the family. He did not want to lose contact with his brother, who was also his best mate, or funnily enough his dad, who he did care for if for no other reason than, he was his dad. In the back of his mind his pampered life was also on the line and there was no point in being hasty and giving that up purely by being impetuous. He grudgingly decided to comply with what he had been told and he would wait for the next message.

He had been in contact with Donna, but sensed her mood had changed of late as she did not seem too keen on seeing him right now; what the fuck was that about? He had demonstrated without doubt what his feelings were and how their relationship was the most important priority in his life. Now he was getting a bit of cold shoulder from her. She said all was good between them and soon they could move on, but for now she had some stuff going on that she had to deal with first. Problem was, he did not have anything to deal with, or even anything to do, as he either sat in at home or went to the gym. That was all he had going on. Consequently, there was plenty of time to think about what his dad was up to and that was not playing out well in his head. His only relief was thinking about Donna and why she was different. Not being able to speak to her was not helping his mental state at all.

The doorbell rang late afternoon and there was Chan restricting the flow of light through the door frame as normal. "Oh." Rich knew this was not a social call. "Well come on in and hit me with what you have been told to say. That's why you are here right, or have you been instructed to literally knock some sense into me?" Rich pulled a chair out and pointed to it for Chan to sit. He did not, he stood very still. "Rich, no slap for you......today. The boss is well pissed off with you, as you can imagine, and has decided to put in play a way to establish how cosied up you and she are. Donna has to decide who suffers for the other night." Rich wanted to speak, but Chan put an end to that in his inimitable style.

"Wait." He said and continued, "The boss figures it will come down to you or her dad, because the kids are obviously out of it and her friend is not really involved. That pretty much leaves you or her old chap. Dog has been out of touch with her for ages, but he is her dad and if he were incapacitated for a while Donna knows she would have a weaker hand. Then there's you. You were the one who pulled her into this, which the boss is sure will play heavily on her thinking, but she has feelings for you and who knows, you could be her future. Before you ask, the hit will be made by some hired help. I'm not sure if the brief is hurt or remove, as I'm not being told that, and it will depend on who she chooses; Russ is making the arrangements." He paused, his eyes went up and to the left as he recalled the conversation with Russ and he made sure he had left nothing out. "Any questions?"

Rich felt ill, a sickening in his gut. Now it made sense why Donna had kept him at arm's length for the last couple of days. She was clearly under orders from Russ to not speak to him about it. He felt useless that she had to go through this on her own as the same no contact directive would have applied to Dog. He looked at Chan, "No questions for you. Chan, you know how much I like you, but with the greatest of respect, can you fuck off out of my flat please as I am not fond of your company today?" Chan nodded to signal his understanding. "Different being on the receiving end I guess," his point was simple, but rapier like. It was not lost on Rich. This was not personal, it was Chan doing what he had done on so many occasions at Rich's behest, so getting too high and mighty was extremely hypocritical. He nodded his head very slowly as this sunk in and then held out his fist for Chan to bump against. He wanted to show he was not holding any grudges. "Rich, I also have to tell you to let Donna decide on her own, so no contact with her. The boss will not like it if you interfere." Rich focused his eyes on Chan's and frowned deeply, "Message received and understood. Now go."

As he shut the door behind Chan, he immediately phoned Donna. No contact my arse, he waited for her to pick up. She did not, so he texted her, *We have to speak call me as soon as you can.* She must be in turmoil as Russ applied his brain crushing technique, which Rich had seen and been a party to so many times. He paced up and down the flat waiting for her to ring.

* * *

From Rich's flat, Chan travelled straight to Dog's home. He rang the bell and a woman, who looked to be in her late twenties, answered it. She opened the door and stepped back in shock at the sight of this huge human being, standing there. Chan was used to this and mostly he milked it for all it was worth. He was just about to speak when the woman shouted back into the house, "This must be for you," and then she moved away leaving him stood there. Dog appeared and bristled; he was instantly in battle mode. "Whoa man." Chan said, "Just here to talk." Dog picked up his coat and made a point of giving Chan a glimpse of the small, nailed club in his pocket and then said, "Outside." Chan took a stride and moved away from the house towards the road, "You not keen on surprise house visits either?" He lobbed this Dog's way.

Once at the road, Dog positioned himself a body length away and had one hand on the club, "What are you here for?" Chan stood across from him, "There is every likelihood me and you will get to dance sometime in the foreseeable future, but not tonight. Chill, let go of the tool and listen up as I have a message from my boss." Dog had no intention of speaking for the sake of it, so he just stared into Chan and held on tightly to the club. This threw Chan a bit, but he continued, "Donna has to decide who pays for the lack of respect shown to Mr. Tomkins the other night and that is likely to be Rich or you, the way he sees it. She has to decide, so no interfering or there will be repercussions." Unlike with Rich, this was being presented with zero feeling and no frills. "Any questions?" Silence from Dog.

As Chan made to make his exit, Dog growled at him,
"You doing the hit?"
"No." Why waste words, was a maxim that had worked very well for Chan for a long time. Dog freed up both hands.
"Paying for that kind of help means he intends to cut someone out permanently. He has not taken this well has he, like the spoilt brat he is. Tell him this; I will be looking over my shoulder and for as long as I'm around he had better do the same. Even if I am taken out he will not be able to relax, because some of my old stir mates will put him down if my girl gets even the slightest bit roughed up through any of this. I've called in a favour or two. He should be far more scared than I'm sure he meant me to be through your visit."

Chan was making no acknowledgement that he would pass the message on or that he had even heard it. He waited for a sensible period, after Dog had stopped talking, before he backed off. These were two tough men, who knew that a confrontation between them was in the offing. Both knew there was unlikely to be a winner, just a lot of pain and injury. They would not back away, but neither was going to force it to happen.

Dog made his way back in and as his lady emerged from the living room, obviously wanting to find out what that was all about. He simply said, "Later," and grabbed his phone. He called Donna and it went unanswered. He texted, *Call me.* Surely now she would let him take control and deal with Danger-Russ once and for all?

* * *

Chan got a safe distance away from Dog's and reported in to Russ how the night had gone. Rich had been visibly shaken by the message, whereas Dog had threatened Russ. Bit stupid, thought Russ, tipping me off like that. He would simply employ a bit more security for the time being until he had dealt with Dog for good. Chan rang off. Russ called Dean to tell him to move in with him for the time being. He removed Dean's protests before they began, "No discussion Dean, you are moving in here for the time being, so I can keep you safe. On your own, you are a complication I do not need, as Dog will use whatever he can to get to me in the same way I would him. Pack your bags and get here tonight." Dean mumbled something about a girl he was with, "Then bring her too, but she can only stay for tonight. OK?" He hung up.

He had stirred things up and now Donna had to show her hand. If she picked Rich, then surely he could see they weren't quite as tight as he had thought. He could influence his son to end it with her, they could get back on track as a family and down the line, once Rich had moved on, she and her old man would get their comeuppance. He would not go through with a slap for Rich as there would be no need, the boy was clearly under her seductive spell and thinking with his cock. This way, he could even save the cost of the extra help.

If she picked Dog, then he would have him taken out permanently, removing her only real bargaining chip. He could then take control of the relationship and assist Rich in seeing it was not right for him to be with a manipulative bitch like her. He swirled the straight Whiskey in the heavy, expensive tumbler and downed it in one. He was pleased with himself. This bump in the road was soon going to be a distant memory and then they could crack on. He would get very close to the boys and let them have more of a say in the business. The closer to him they were, the less likely this crap was going to happen again. He sat back in his winged chair, put his feet on the stool and enjoyed the after burn of his single malt.

CHAPTER 24.

The time is always right to do what is right. - Martin Luther King, Jr.

She texted both Rich and her Dad the same message; *Can you meet me at the Red Lion for 1pm?* They had both replied with a yes and again both had tried to ring her, but she wanted this done face to face with all three of them in attendance. The kids would be at school and if she got stupidly delayed then Layla had agreed to pick them up for her. She had swapped a half shift at the shop and was free to meet up. First, she called in to see PD and explained her predicament.

"I'm meeting with dad and Rich this lunchtime to tell them what I have decided and to keep them both in line. All that male bravado let loose and the kids could be in trouble, so I will get them on a short leash as I'm sure from what Chan said that dad has already gone against what I asked. You are quite welcome to come along, BUT I would rather you did not. You, you silly old sod, mean the world to me and I can never forgive myself for getting you mixed up in this, so if I can keep you out of it from now on, it will make me feel so much better." PD looked a bit hurt, "Too old and feeble to be near a beating, am I?" She squeezed his forearm, "No. Too important to me to get damaged, that's why. I promise if I need you I will shout, but at present I have it under control, I think!" He put his hand on hers, "OK then, if that's how you want it. That Chan can consider himself a lucky boy not having to face me." He let fly with a couple of jabs.

They shared a look. "I am quite prepared to be the scapegoat you know," he said and with a tear in her eye, she gave him a huge hug. "I know, I know." She gripped him tight for a few more seconds and then let go. "However, I do not need Russ to beat you up..........as I could do that myself," she leapt away as he grabbed at a towel to swipe her with. "No being too clever missy with whatever it is you are thinking. Anyway, if I'm not coming to the pub you can tell me before you go...."

* * *

Dog was at the Red Lion first and ordered himself a pint and was just about to pay when Rich arrived. It was awkward between them, as they were still relative strangers, but Dog broke the ice and bought Rich a drink. Donna was what they had in common, at least that was all they knew about at that time. After the first, long sup, they were about to engage in some idle chat, when Donna appeared. She was dressed in tight, faded blue jeans, with a faux leather biker jacket, over a low cut, white T-shirt. She had chosen her clothes with an intention to accentuate her figure and looks. Her hair was down, which was unusual as she was mostly sporting a pony tail, and her makeup had been done; not too much, but with purpose and to good effect. Layla had helped her, and she had to admit the girl next door had done her proud. Looking good was all part of being ready to face Russ. He might not give a stuff, but it was all part of some feminine suit of armour.

Dog ordered her a drink and Rich kissed and then hugged her. Dog looked at Rich, "She's not been answering your calls either I take it?" Rich got his phone out, "Want to see how many times I have been rejected? I have been going crazy, why didn't you pick up or at least text back?" Donna was seated now, and she sipped her still mineral water through the straw provided. "Because, it was my problem and I wanted the space to decide what to do without any distractions, or well-intended input, swaying my thoughts. Before you both sulk, can I say I have made it OK to this point without any machismo from you dad. Rich, let's not talk about what your input has led to." The men looked at each other and then at Donna. "So," said Dog, "Can I say that the only sensible option is to let me loose and I will clear this whole pile of shit up in a couple of days." Rich jumped in, "I will go and have it out with my dad, just as I said on the night of the fight. I can make him see that we are good together. Anyway, there is no way he will want to cut me out of his life, so he will see sense."

Donna just stared at her dad and then at Rich, disbelieving what she had just heard. "Well thank my lucky stars I did not involve either of you in what to do about this. Dad, if you cause Russ any harm, how do you think Rich and you are ever going to have a relationship? If we make it beyond all this crap, I hope you know that will be important to me. Rich, your dad is an angry, impetuous man and right now there is a serious likelihood you will not be part of the family or the business going forward. I certainly do not want you begging and pleading on my behalf. Plus, he may well chuck you out of the business, but he is not going to do any permanent damage to you. That means my dad is being lined up to take the fall for this. Having just got to get to know him all over again, I would like him to be around for a while. I'm sorry to be blunt, but your thinking is rubbish." Dog smirked at Rich, "Yours too," his head shot back, and the smirk was gone. "Thank you both for trying, but I have already decided what I will do."

She sipped again through the straw and both were focusing all their attention on her. They waited to hear what she had to say, but she was not saying anything. Rich broke the silence,
"Well, tell us then." She looked from one to the other,

"Nope."

"What?" they chorused together.

"Now listen here my girl, if you think I'm going to let you walk out of here without me knowing what you have got up your sleeve, then you are very much mistaken."

Donna looked at her dad and gently shook her head in semi irritation,

"What are you going to do then, physically restrain me? Once you apologise for being such a prat and thinking you can take control over my decisions, when you have been a non-existent in my life for so long, then I will tell you what you can do for me." She looked away, her annoyance clear, and spoke to Rich,

"IF, we are going to have a life together then you realise right now that you do not tell me what to do or try to rule over me. Got it?" he nodded and looked into his drink. She turned back to Dog,

"Well?" He folded his arms and sat back. "Either you apologise right now, or you have no part in the rest of this sleazy little tale." She turned an ear to him, "I did not hear that." He shuffled in his seat,

"OK then, 'sorry'," said in a condescending manner.

"That will have to do," she said. "Now stop being babies the pair of you as this is what is going to happen."

"I have a proposal for Russ that I am going to deliver to him right after I leave here, the exact details of which you do not need to know just yet. Rich, this is going to be hard for you, but please understand my reasons. Dad, if he reacts badly to what I have said, and you think the kids might be in any sort of danger, then do whatever you have to that will keep them out of his reach. They are the priority in all this as they are totally innocent and need a break, not more shit. I do not care who you trample on, you protect them? Got it?" He barely moved his head, but the nod of agreement was there, if not total harmony with what she was doing. "Rich, if I'm killed or put out of action for a long time, I want you to help dad and that will mean going against your family and all you have known. If you feel the same way about me, as I do you, then if anyone hurt you I could not be associated with them. I am presuming that is how it is for you."

He was not liking this one little bit. The strain and unease were etched across his facial features. Whatever she had planned she knew Russ might not look kindly on it and yes, his old fellah was quite capable of authorising the ultimate penalty on her. She was preparing them for the worst. He grabbed her hand. "I hope you know what you are doing, because it all sounds one big gamble to me and all I know is I do not want to lose you for a second, let alone forever. I am going along with your wishes, because, as you have already told me so gently, I probably do not have a better alternative, but you come back to me." He was struggling through the emotion in his voice, but just about held it together. They hugged, and tears rolled down her face. She let go of his frame, but kept a tight grip on his hand, "Dad, do not touch a hair on his head. I love him." Dog could see the closeness between them and he said, "Spoilsport." He grinned at Rich and Donna slapped his shoulder, "Behave."

She picked up her drink and said, "To a week's time, when we'll all be sat here with all our own teeth," they clinked glasses and drank, "A week's time." Dog was the most relaxed of them all as he had been in many scrapes in his time, "Does it matter that most of my teeth have been knocked out already?" Nervous grins. It was not funny, but it helped release some of the pent-up pressure. "Right then, I'm off to meet Mr. Tomkins, so have your phones on and I will call you both later. Wish me luck." Her attempted brave face scarcely covered the fear she was exuding in her voice and mannerisms as she left the table, "I love you both." Then she was gone, before any more emotion could take hold. She needed to ready herself for the confrontation with Russ.

CHAPTER 25.

You can't deny who you are, so you might as well be yourself in the most authentic way. – Ben Hopkins.

There was every possibility she would be in for a severe beating today or even worse. Body and mind prepare us in the same way for both, as the severity is not the important part. Going back through many ancestral people, our pre-conditioned response to a stressful or dangerous situation will evidence itself through butterflies, sweating, shakes and of course little voices in our head contradicting each other about just how bad things could be. 'You will be fine' to 'You are going to die'. As she turned the corner into the road where Russ kept his office, Donna was close to throwing up, as her stomach reacted to the signals her brain was sending. Outside the building she noticed a couple of men, just sitting in a big, black car. She could not make out too much detail about them as the reflections on the car windows made that difficult, but they were big men judging by the large, dark shapes their outlines made. As she drew nearer, she could see both were in sunglasses. It was no coincidence that these two, were parked near to where Russ based himself. He had his muscle close by and intentionally, they were not being inconspicuous about their presence.

At the entrance, she stopped walking and took a couple of big deep breaths, wiped her sweaty palms on her jeans, shook her arms and legs out and pulled herself up to her full height. Final preparations as she readied herself to march in there confidently. Much of this same calming strategy was used as she left her dressing room for the ring, because whilst most fighters liked to be hyped up, she preferred to be very relaxed. That kept her senses alert. Many opponents had charged out wildly throwing punches, she just dodged them and made telling, accurate and damaging blows of her own. No point wasting energy through emotion. Her controlled approach suited her and against these pumped up boxers, so often she was immediately in control of the contest.

Today, however, would be different. Russ was likely to be calm and cocky to begin with and it was only as the discussion progressed that he might lose it. However, she was not going through her calming routine for him, this was all for her. She had to stay sharp and not make any silly errors that could prove costly in so many ways. She circled her neck left and then right, shook her shoulders and opened the door to his reception area. There was his receptionist.

"Can I help?" she asked. "I would like to see Russ, Mr. Tomkins, please? Before you ask, no I do not have an appointment, but he is expecting me to be in touch. My name is Donna." As she picked up the phone she indicated for Donna to take a seat on one of two leather sofas. "There's a Donna here to see you..................... OK.... yeah.... thanks," she replaced the phone and looked at Donna, "He is in the middle of something, but he said you should wait for him." More mind games, thought Donna. In any normal reception the person behind the counter would smile, offer a drink, make sure they were OK to wait and perhaps engage in a few pleasantries. Not here. Her job was not to make people feel comfortable. Those who visited Russ were more likely to be here at his bidding, either to discuss a favour he needed or for a friendly chat that was going to be anything but. She looked around the room and it was stark. No pictures or posters, pale cream floor tiles, magnolia walls and a modern grey desk for his receptionist to sit behind on a grey, cloth covered office chair. No computer even. Stupid, Donna thought to herself, of course no computer as that would mean records and they in turn meant tax bills or possible incrimination.

Well, if she was going to sit here for who knew how long, she was going to fill the time.
"Don't you get bored?" she asked the receptionist.
"Do you know Mr. Tomkins very well?" was the unexpected retort given in a serious way with quite a stony look on her face.
"So, so."
"I see. Well if you did, you would know that he doesn't really 'do' boring and would not want his staff to describe anything to do with him as such." Donna admonished herself; she had judged this girl on her trim body and nice looks and made a judgement about why Russ had employed her. Shame on you, she thought, this was someone proud of what they were doing and hopefully making a decent living out of it. Who was she to judge? She stood up and offered a hand.
"Let's start over, I'm Donna." Hand accepted and shook.
"I'm Carly." Still little expression in evidence.
"I was not meaning to be rude or anything, I just noticed you had no computer, so I wondered how you kept busy. Sorry, I did not mean to annoy you." The expression thawed a little, but nothing coming back yet.

"I am here, because Mr. Tomkins is not happy with me as I inadvertently messed up a deal of his, well a deal of sorts anyway. Like most people you encounter here I suppose, he is displeased with me and I would rather talk to someone than sit there and think about what will happen when he finishes whatever it is he's doing. That is why I am talking crap and being annoying." At last a response, "I see tough men, really tough looking men, shaking in their boots waiting for Mr. Tomkins, so I think you are doing well playing it this cool. You're the boxer, right?" Donna was so relieved to have a way of passing some time, so she could quieten her inner dialogue.

"Yeah. Thanks, by the way, but trust me I am bricking it," and revealed more than she intended as she opened her eyes wide and rubbed her neck nervously.

Chan entered and stopped mid-stride as he caught sight of Donna, then quickly regained his distinctive gait and headed through another door. He made no acknowledgement of Carly at all, no look, no brief wave of a hand, nothing.
"Smooth bugger isn't he," Donna said. Carly gave a warm smile.
"He's lovely really, a big pussycat." Donna gave a surprised look,
"When he's not beating the hell out of some poor mug you mean." They shared a laugh.
"There is that, but he does what he does for pay, not pleasure, and I see too many minders with a psychopath edge to them." Donna folded her arms.
"So, if he gets me in a headlock later I should drop him a fiver to stop, should I?" Carly beamed wide.
"I'm not sure he's a headlock type and Mr. Tomkins can probably beat your pay offer I'm guessing. Speak as you find and all I know is Chan has only ever been nice to me and yes, the same does go for Mr. Tomkins, although I do know he has a side of him to avoid. You will be getting me in trouble."

With that she looked at a couple of pieces of paper on her desk and glanced at her phone as if to indicate conversation over.
"You are right, sorry; again. I will not lead you down any dark path, I promise." She placed her hand on her heart. "You look like you take care of yourself, so what's your fitness regime?" Carly was visibly pleased by the comment.
"I play Netball for a team and I'm really into Yoga." Donna nodded her approval,
"That's quite a mixture."
"Well, my ex-boyfriend said Netball was because I liked to flash my knickers at the boys in school. But he was a twot," she paused to gently tap Donna's extended hand in a sign of female unity. "In truth I love being with the girls and we have a great social life around the training and matches. It keeps me relatively fit. The Yoga I used to do with my gran, when I went round hers as a kid, and then I grew to love it."

Donna was enjoying the chat and was about to carry on when the door opened and there was Chan where the opening used to be. He did not speak, he just raised one hand to half way up his body and then beckoned her once by curling his fingers towards his palm. Normally, she would have some wisecrack to make, but this was not the time. Anyway, she needed to focus, and focus good, for the duel to come. She was enough together in her thinking to realise that what Russ had been doing, was to wait for Chan before he saw her; but why? She might be a decent boxer, but she was no match for Russ in any form of combat that was clear. Besides, he probably had bars, knives and even guns in there. So, why did he need Chan to be in attendance? There go those voices again; was that good for her or bad news?

She moved through the door, as Chan stepped aside, and followed him the short walk to where Russ sat in his office. The chair back was facing her, and he was reclining in it as she entered. When he turned his fingers were steepled and he looked beyond smug. There are people you encounter who only need to say 'Hello' and you will find it irritating. Russ was that person to her. That superior look, slick suit & tie and those bloody fingers! "Most people make an appointment to see me, you're lucky I was in." She could see he was delighting in this opening encounter. He stopped. He is waiting for me to get gobby, so let's disappoint him. "Thank you for seeing me." His face was slowly moving from brash to more serious. "At our last 'extremely enjoyable' meeting I asked you to provide me with a name of someone close to you, who you felt should bear the brunt for you making me lose face and causing me untold embarrassment. Do you have a name for me?" She swallowed.

Shit, that was a giveaway she was scared; get a grip woman.

"Yes." Pause. "Do not fuck with me girl, who is it?" She held her head high and said, "Donna Wilbraham."

Russ looked at her. Then he looked at Chan. Then back at Donna. His unfolding displeasure being given away by the redness rising up his face and the arrival of some veins in his neck and forehead she was sure were not there a minute ago. He rose from his seat quickly and slammed his hand into the desktop so loudly she thought it might break in two. She jumped as the sound of the slam rung out around the room. Then he was motionless, just leaning on his arms. After what seemed an age, he lifted his eyes and fixed them on a point on the wall close to the right of Donna's head. "I thought I said, do not fuck with me." Tread carefully, she was telling herself, this fucker is going to blow if you are not mindful of everything you say. If Goliath was not in front of that door, making a run for it would definitely seem a good option right now. Steady, steady, you've been practising and know the words so well, just say them and then it's up to him what happens.

"It was my mess up, so why should I not suffer for it? Despite whatever you may think, I love my dad and let's face it, if I had picked him there was a chance he would seek revenge for whatever you did to him. We both know that means you might have gone beyond sending him to A & E. I could not live with being responsible for that. I love Rich and there is no 'us' if I chose him. Neither of them or anyone else I know had a thing to do with what happened, so that leaves me."

Russ motioned to move round the desk and Chan stepped forward. Here we go she thought and instinctively raised her hands in a boxer's guard. However, Chan was moving between Russ and her. Russ looked up, realised what Chan was doing, stopped and moved back behind his desk. He gestured with his hand for Chan to resume his position near the door. That's why he had waited, he could not trust himself to refrain from setting about her there and then if his temper took hold. For some reason Chan was there to make sure that did not happen. But why? Perhaps this was not where they took care of business such as this or perhaps he might have actually killed her and then been up for a hefty stint at her majesty's pleasure. She was not sure why, but she was relieved and dropped her hands and waited for whatever was going to happen next.

Russ was standing, staring out of the window, rubbing his face with his hands as he regained a semblance of composure. "I am certain that in coming to this decision it would not have escaped you I knew all of that crap you just came out with. That was why I dumped it on you." He turned round and she was unsure whether she was meant to say anything or not, but he made it quite clear, "DO NOT say a fucking thing whilst I think." He seemed lost in thought for a minute and then stormed out of the room, door banging in its hinges as he left. Chan was still in the room with her, but he was not saying anything. "Can I call......," he did not wait for the sentence to end, he just gave one small shake of his head to left, then right and then back to the centre.

She had given the kids a massive hug this morning, as they left for school, and they had both looked at her as if to say, 'What's up with you?', She began wondering when she would get to do that again, if ever. She had totally cocked this up. Dad will probably get taken out completely. Rich will be out of the family and chances are with a smack. Her immediate future looked like being in either the hospital or the mortuary. She could feel herself shaking through fright and nerves and paced about a bit to try and ease these natural responses to impending peril.

Russ was gone for ages and not one word was passed between her and Chan; he really was good at his job and well-practiced in this. The silence had added to her severe discomfort in mind, body and probably her soul too. Russ returned. His facial colour was back to normal and he had an air of calm. "I asked you for a name and you have decided to play games with me...." She spoke up, "I have not played ga...." In a loud, assertive voice, he said, "Shut the fuck up. I have the power to hurt a lot of people you love, so it would be unwise to push me. I speak, you listen. End of." He grabbed at his tie knot and stretched his neck out of his shirt and then continued. "It is not clever to play games with me when lives are on the line, but if that is how you want it, so be it. I have made a call. Someone close to you will get it tonight. Not my Rich, not your dad. Someone really close to you."

Her mind was racing.

If not Dog or Rich, then who? Someone really close to me, he said. Think woman, think. He cannot mean..................

She screamed uncontrollably at him, "No, you can't. They are only kids." Without really thinking she began to move towards him, to do what, she had no idea.

However, she was going nowhere as Chan had his hands on both shoulders from behind. "I can, and I have. Get out of here. You might want to say 'sorry' for being the cause of what is coming. That is all you can do, as the hit is in place. Now you listen carefully." She was sobbing and fighting against Chan's grip without any effect, but with absolute hate in her eyes as she looked at Russ. "You are responsible for this. Live with that. Tomorrow, will be a bad day for you. If you don't want any more days like that, within one week you come back to see me and this time I want a name of someone other than you. Now fuck off." Chan gripped even tighter and she felt herself moving as he used his muscle to walk her out of the office, through reception and into the road outside.

"How can you work for that monster?" she shouted at him, "You are no better than he is Chan. Children? Is that what you do?" As he let go she went for him, but he was a big guy and her wild punches were not going to have any impact. Then he shoved her away from him. He did not look his normal self; had she touched a nerve or perhaps he was uncomfortable with what had just happened. "I had no idea what he was doing." Then he went back inside. "Blood on your hands too, if this happens," she called after him.

CHAPTER 26.

"Children are not distractions from more important work. They are the most important work." – C S Lewis.

She grabbed her phone and rang her dad, "Get to the kids quickly, he's going after the kids." He started to ask questions, but she stopped him short and shrieked into the phone, "Just go."

Then she rang Rich, "He is going to kill the kids, can you stop him? Do something Rich, he cannot hurt either of them." Rich was stunned, "He couldn't. He won't..." she stopped him, "I have to go as I'm meeting dad with the kids and if they're OK we'll have to figure out what to do. All I know is I was in the meeting and I know what that devil of a father of yours said, so get off the phone and sort him out. Bye," with that she hung up. Her head was mush and she was openly crying in absolute terror at what he had said was going to happen. Children get hurt, because some wanker is unhappy a stage managed fight did not go as planned? What absurd and mixed up world did they live in? First thing was to get to them and then consider how to keep them safe. She could not get her head beyond just seeing them again.

* * *

As she approached the school, she saw her dad at the gates with Layla and the kids. Thank Christ for that, they were safe, for now at least. She gathered them both up in her arms and wept. "Are you both OK?" her voice was excited and unnerving them, "We are fine," said Maggie, "Why, what's the matter?" Layla gently tugged at Donna to let them loose and squinted her eyes at her friend to let her know to stop this pouring out of emotion. It was not helping anyone and certainly not two young children. She grabbed a hand of each and said, "They've been saying hello to granddad, haven't you kids?" They both seemed a little in shock by Donna's actions, but Sam said, "Yeah. He's called Dog; is that right?" A quick, frowned look from Donna to her dad and back to the kids, "I think we will go with Granddad, don't you? I think you deserve a treat?" They looked at each other and then at Donna, "What for?" Donna gave Layla some money, "For being brilliant. That good enough? Layla will take you to that shop and we'll wait outside for you." As they happily skipped off, she wiped her eyes,

"Thanks dad. Sorry to be so hysterical on the phone, but I was so worried. We are not done yet as he's ordered a hit on one or both of them." Dog put his arm round her shoulder and they slowly ambled to the shop. "You sure about this, because he is getting into some crazy territory if he's going to start paying for kids to get whacked?" She moved out from under his arm and faced him. "The way my brain is at this precise second, I could have imagined the whole thing, but he told me that someone close to me was going to get it. He had put the wheels in motion for tonight. He said not you or Rich, someone really close to me and he did not bat an eyelid when I screamed at him about the kids. What are we going to do?" This was Dog's world and he did not seem fazed at all.

"No point in running, because then you can never stop, and we have to keep life as normal as possible for those kids. I will stay at yours tonight. If anyone comes with shooters we are all as good as done for, but anything less and they will not get by me. I promise you that."

* * *

Rich phoned his dad;

"Dad?"
"You rang my number, so who did you expect?"
"Is this true?"
"What?"
"That you have put a contract out on those kids?"
"Since when do I answer to you?"
"Fuck all that. Have you?"
"Careful Rich, I'm not in a great frame of mind and certainly not best pleased with you, so I would avoid pissing me off any further if I were you."
"Call it off dad. Please. Before it is too late. Killing children, is that the level we are at now?"
"Stop your whining and listen. Your 'girlfriend' thought she could play games with Russ Tomkins and now she is learning you can't. I had to show her that if she does, if anyone does, they pay for it. As she would not give me a name, I have chosen for her. That is all you need to know."
"Dad, you have made your point, now call it off."
"Can't. The contract is with a couple of pro's from out of town I sorted through a third party and I have no idea how to contact them. That's if I even wanted to."

"Know this dad. I will be with Donna and those kids tonight, so if these guys are going to earn their money they may well have to take me out too."
"Rich, you have made your bed, try not to die in it."

Russ hung up. Rich knew how callous his father could be, but he was incredulous that he could care so little for his own son that he accepted putting him in harm's way was more important than losing respect. Was there any way back for them now as father and son? Then he realised how self-centred he was being, as he had momentarily forgotten that his dad was about to be responsible for the death of a child, or possibly even two. This was not his father, not the dad he knew. Whilst deep down he was only too aware that Russ was capable of some barbaric and cruel acts, this was a whole new level. Had he lost it? Was it the Donna situation that had pushed him over or was there something else going on?

Right now, he had to get to Donna's flat and do what he could to help protect her and the family. Then he would need to find out where Dean stood in all this. He was starting to resign himself to losing his dad as part of his life, but his brother too? All that was immaterial if he did not survive this night.

* * *

Back at the flat, Donna sat Maggie and Sam down at the kitchen table with their sweets and took all the adults into the other room.

"They must know nothing about what is going on, so watch what you say and treat this as an ordinary night. Got it?"

Layla piped up, "Ordinary! Other than you are acting like a crazy woman, their long lost granddad has not only turned up but is staying the night, as am I even though I live next door, oh and the man you called a pervert is also coming to join the stopover. Yeah, just a bog standard night at Donna's I'd say."

"Well how do you expect me to act?" Donna was being irrational and understandably so, but Layla was right and raised voices were doing the opposite of what Donna had asked for. Dog, jumped in.

"Can I suggest something?" Donna looked away, crossing her arms as she did so. Layla looked ready to cry. Both were scared and needed calming down. "We should distract them, so they don't have a chance to sense any of what we might be giving off. What do they like doing most?"
"Disney. They are kids."

"Right, pick out a film and we all get in there and watch it, perhaps even another one, until they are too tired. I will stay close to the door, in case, and you two grab one each to sit with. How does that sound?"

Nods and a slight thawing of the frost between them. Donna holds a hand out and Layla gently taps it. Dog cannot help but notice and continues. "You know what they say at Disney parks, 'On Show', so come on you two, get in there like it's Christmas Eve. No idea what lover boy will do when he comes, but...."
"Rich. His name is Rich, not 'lover boy'. He is choosing to be with me tonight, so YOU will make him welcome." She prodded her dad in the chest with one finger of her right hand.
"Where's he sleeping?"
"Are you seriously telling me that with all we have going on, and having only just started to get to know me again, you are worried about that? Funnily enough dad, I doubt anyone is feeling overly randy tonight, so nothing to trouble your head about. I appreciate you being here and I'm pleased we are back on good terms, but do not think you will have any say on who I sleep with." They glare at each other. Layla steps between them;
"For fuck's sake, this is all getting silly. Donna, go and get a film on," and with that she pushed her mate towards the door. "Anyway, you speak for yourself, I am as randy as hell; you will need to watch yourself later Dog." He grinned, like most men would, he took it as a compliment. She was shoving Donna through the door when he called out, "Sorry." Donna's head popped back through the door, "Me too. I am so pleased you are here tonight." One more push from Layla and she was gone. Layla turned to Dog, "I was only joking, so stop looking at my arse."
"I was not, I mean if I was, I didn't mean to......"

She grinned at how uncomfortable he was, this hard man she had heard about from Donna. As he looked up and saw her, he realised he'd been had.
"You, horrible cow."
"That's right and now we both have animal names. Come on," her head beckoned him to follow.

Maggie and Sam loved 'The Lion King', even though they had seen it so many times already. The brilliance and splendour of Simba and Nala, meant they were oblivious to the fidgeting of fingers Donna was preoccupied with all the way through. Let alone all the other giveaways that betrayed how on edge all the adults were. When Rich arrived, Donna let him in. She immediately took him into the other room for a 'briefing' on how he was to behave whilst the kids were up and to not get clever with her dad. "What do you mean? Why?" She waved a finger at him in response, "Just do not. Everyone is uptight and prickly. For tonight, I need calm waters."

* * *

The night passed quietly. The kids went to bed as usual, Dog slept on the couch, Rich on the chair and Layla jumped in bed with Donna;

"Donna? Remember earlier when I said I felt a little randy." Layla gently stroked Donna's hair. Thank God she's here, because without her stupid little jokey comments, this night would have felt much longer. The adrenaline had given her extra verve to keep the one liners coming.

"Touch me and die."
"Oh Donna, you gorgeous creature, resistance is futile."
"Oh Layla, you idiot, carrying on will be fatal."
"OK then, but that only leaves your boyfriend or your dad to satisfy me......... or both."
"Best if you leave them to be alert. Night Layla, now try and get to sleep."
"Night Donna......................... I bet I can keep them alert."
"Night Layla."

* * *

Donna hardly slept and when she did it was for brief periods, but during one of these her mobile rang, scaring the bejeezus out of her and Layla. She collected herself. As it was light, it was clearly morning, so she checked the time and saw it was just after 6.33am. Groggily she answered it.

"Yup, hullo."
"Yeah, it's Donna."
"Tommy?"
Her face drained and she sat up, instantly awake and animated.
"Say that again."
"How?"
She listened.
"Are they sure?"
"OK, ok, yeah, sorry." She ended the call and looked at Layla.

"PD is dead."

She fell against her friend and open mouthed, she let out a long, almost silent scream. She shook and jerked with the outpouring of emotion. The tears flowed as she limply held on to Layla's solid embrace.

"I didn't even think about him last night and now he's dead." She let go and anguish pained her features. "It's because of me."

CHAPTER 27.

I will swallow my blood before I swallow my pride. - Al Capone.

The Police did some preliminary investigations and for a couple of days the gym was a crime scene, with the detectives looking for clues. They did not find any. The location of the gym meant there was no CCTV on premises anywhere near that might have helped. Inside, the ransacked office suggested a robbery gone wrong. The cause of death was announced as a blow to the head with a heavy object, which had been identified as a moulded dumbbell. They reasoned that PD was on his own, when person, or persons, unknown entered and attacked him. They were probably after a quick steal to fund a drug habit or pay for some booze.

Chances were, they did not mean to kill him, they just needed him quiet whilst they looked for whatever would provide them with a fast sale and faster access to a fix. It was a boxing gym, so they would not take the chance of him putting up a fight. They would have been looking to put him to sleep for a while, whilst they sought any useful gear, but they hit him too hard.

A Detective Sergeant, wearing a lived-in suit with a tie pulled loose over an undone top button, met with some of the senior 'kids' from the gym and explained what they had found. It was highly unlikely they would find the perpetrator, because nothing had been taken. Perhaps they realised he was dead and legged it. If anything came to light they should contact him. He expressed his sympathy, but it was cold and delivered as a professional curtesy as opposed to with any real feeling. This man had never met PD, so what else would they expect? They asked him a couple of questions, but it was pointless;

"Why would anyone target a run-down boxing gym for a snatch?"
"These type of criminals, do not necessarily think too much about it. Who knows, could just be they happened to be passing and the door was open."

"What will you do now to catch them?"
"The investigation will remain open for the time being, but we have no leads to follow up on at present. As and when new information becomes available, it will be processed."

"Is that it then? PD is dead man; DEAD! His killer is still wandering around and you have no idea who he is. That's shit."
"We have carried out a full investigation. In terms of forensic evidence there is nothing to assist our enquiries; no break-in, the weapon used was a piece of this gym's equipment, no CCTV and by all accounts this was a man without enemies. I understand your frustration, I really do, but we have other cases to investigate."

It was all delivered void of emotion. Quite obviously it was a well voiced speech this sergeant had to make on a regular basis. Too many crimes, not enough police officers and they would prioritise those they felt there was headway to be made in. If the victim was not to do with you, that approach made perfect sense. But, if you had an emotional attachment then you wanted the world to stop until justice was done. Police resourcing was someone else's problem and to everyone connected with the gym this case was the only priority, so stop all this crap and go find the killer.

Tommy was looked upon as the senior fighter at the gym, due to his close bond with PD and his length of service. He called an end to the questioning. It was getting them nowhere and the only result was to further stoke the anger and bitterness everyone was feeling. The copper left.

If everyone was prepared to chip in, Tommy would take over from PD for the time being until a long term solution was found. Everyone assembled knew one possible solution was the gym closing. They all agreed. Get the funeral over and then re-open the gym. Donna could not bring herself to attend the meeting with the Police, so Tommy called her afterwards, as he did anyone who did not make it. He relayed the conversation and what had been agreed. Donna experienced the same resentment as the rest when she heard the investigation was more or less over no sooner than it had begun. In addition, she felt the crushing heaviness of guilt. It was no coincidence that Russ had put out a hit on someone close to her and then PD gets a visit from 'druggies', apparently. She had been so pre-occupied with keeping Maggie & Sam safe, that she had not stopped to think who else he could look to hurt her through.

The grief was unbearable. PD was a huge part of her life and had influenced her way beyond what he taught her to do with boxing. He had made her a better person, no doubt about it, just as he had anyone who attended his establishment if they were sensible enough to listen to him. Piled on top of that was how her thoughts went from PD to Helen and why she had to suffer the loss of two such close people at her tender age. What was it PD used to say? "There is no such thing as 'fair' in this world. The sooner you understand that, the better for you." Right again old man, you are right again. What she needed was to curl up in a little ball for days on end to come to terms with the death of PD. Perhaps this was also the time to pay 'grief' its dues for Helen, as that was long overdue. Easily said, but how could she? Life does not stop for a nine year old and a seven year old. As they had not known PD that well, his passing was thankfully only laying the lightest touch on them. Any sorrow they experienced was mostly through the effect it was having on Donna. PD did not visit the flat very often and when they were out of school he was tending his gym, so the odd meet up happened, but it would be wrong to say they were close.

The kids were, as always, the number one priority, but now she had so much more to deal with. Rich and her had spoken, but she could not think about their relationship right now. He was a part of Russ and all that meant. Rich was going to see his dad and have it out, but so what? PD was dead and gone from her life. Then there was her dad. As delicately as he was capable of being, he made it known that had he been allowed to take control of things, PD might still be around. He was asking for her approval for him to be let loose and take care of everything. He was certainly persistent in asking. Her head was brimming with so much stuff that she could not think straight, other than to know she was not thinking straight. Making decisions now was not a good idea.

Layla knew what was needed and she dropped her air head, funny girl act to organise everything. She spoke to Donna and began by saying she was not taking no as an answer. She would swap flats with Donna for the time being and look after Maggie and Sam. That would give Donna some space to think or grieve or just stare into space if that was what it took. Dog would be kept on the leash as he could help with the kids; he could not refuse that. Rich, well if absence does make the heart grow fonder a few days away from each other would tell them a lot about the sustainability of their love. The beauty being she was next door, so there was a hug, a chat or any other emotional support she needed a step away, but the day to day baggage was gone. The funeral was in three days' time and they could discuss 'what now?' then.

* * *

Rich had tried to speak to his dad on the phone, but clearly the old man was not answering; more stupid bloody mind games. So, he considered going to the house early one morning, but with how things were between them, that did not feel right. He would go to his office and see him there.

As he parked, he noticed that security had been stepped up as there were a few new faces in cars close by.

He asked Carly if Russ was in and she said yes, but he had someone coming to see him in an hour. "Cancel it," he said and marched through the connecting door to the small corridor leading to where Russ worked. He opened the door and faced Russ who was chatting to Chan.

"Dad, we need to talk."
"Do we now?"
"Yes, we do. Did you kill Donna's coach?"
"Son. Sit down. If you continue to bark at me like that, Chan will help you find your way out, but not before I have shown you I am still too much of a man for you to gob off at. Clear?"
Rich sits down and looks scolded.
"OK. Sorry. What the fuck is going on dad?"
"You know perfectly well what is going on. Why are you here?"
"I have found someone I really care about, and I do not want to let her go. But you have killed her coach and someone who was also a very close friend. Rumour was you were going to kill two young kids and all to teach her a lesson. I am here to try and find a way to resolve my differences with you and find a way forward for me and Donna."

Russ dips back his chair and steeples his fingers.
"Let me point out that you and Dean are at the root of all this, because I would never have known of this girl without you two 'introducing' me to her. Next, I have no idea what one of my sons sees in a piece of skirt from the ghetto's, as you could clearly do better. I made a choice about having someone in my life and I hoped you would have realised why and followed my example, but who knows what is going on with you right now." He leant forward, and a different look came over him; more serious. He glared at Rich.

"Your lady friend thought I could be pissed about with, so I sent her a warning to show I could not. He was meant to be bruised and the odd rib broken, but they hit him with some dumbbell from behind and that was it. I am sorry, as I liked PD, but this is all her fault. I never said anything about hurting kids, she said that, and I let her think it."
"Would you have hurt them?"
Russ paused and then very deliberately said,
"As you should know by now, I will do whatever I think is right to maintain order on my streets. Push me and I will snap your neck, that is what has worked and continues to work."
"Dad, to save face you have had a man killed and I am not sure if you would have resorted to killing children. This was not a major deal or anything of importance, it was to stop a few irrelevant faces from thinking you were losing your grip. Can you hear what you are saying?"
"Are you telling me how to run my business? I think my long life in this line of work suggests I know more than you. Here is something else to think on. I asked her for a name and she played games. I am telling you what I told her, if she did not pick then I would, but she would still need to give me a name or it would go on until she did. I

will take every person she loves off the face of this earth if I need to."
"Does that include me? Does that include kids?"
"Anyone and everyone until I am satisfied. You need to decide if you are with me. Are you capable of being my son and living life as someone who needs to get their hands dirty every so often." He was getting heated and impassioned in volume and expression.

Rich was taken aback. However he had envisaged this chat going, it had not been like this.
"You are right dad, I do need to decide." He rose to leave. Russ spoke up again, this time he was more devious in his modulation. If you want to come in here and ball at me, I think I should leave you with something to mull over.
"I might see you at the funeral."
"Dad, you cannot be serious."
"Why not? It will be an ideal time to see if your 'girlfriend' has a name for me."
"Let this go for fuck's sake."
"I will let go once order is restored and everyone knows I am still the man and not to be fucked with."
"Everyone does know that, carrying on with this is pointless."
"I will decide when I pull the plug and right now I think there is still a message to get out there."

Rich looked at Chan, who was free from any outward expression of sentiment. He glanced back at his dad, shook his head and was then gone.

"What about that Chan, my own son thinking he knows better than me about how to run a firm like this. Can you believe it? Not like Rich to get infatuated with a bit of pussy, but I guess lust can do strange things to a man." He looked at Chan and knew something was not right.

"What's up?"
"Boss, you said to tell you when I was ready to move on. I am telling you. You have a few extra boys around you, so now seems a good time."
"Why?"
"The fact you do not know why, tells me you are not the Russ Tomkins you were. PD was a good man and you hired amateurs to go after him. I liked him. He deserved better than to be contracted out to incompetents. More of a worry for me, is that you do not seem to be able to say that kids are not beyond a bit of your punishment. This matter is out of hand and being driven by ego. That is not the business I am in or want to be associated with."
"You leave me, and you leave my protection. Think carefully."
"I have. I hope we can leave on OK terms boss. Please, do not threaten me again." Chan lifted himself off the chair and left the room. Those conversations in such a short space of time would have made most rational people reflect on what they were

doing and consider if a change of tack was required. Russ was not most people and who could say if he was being rational or not. Like many who are in charge of an organisation for a long while, they can become detached from the view of those they work with and believe approval is a given. It may well be at surface level, but dig a little and there is resentment or disillusionment waiting, just waiting, for the time to air itself. Fuck 'em all, he thought without a hint of self-doubt. However, he had one more meeting yet and that was to shake him more than he could possibly imagine.

* * *

Chan phoned both Dean and Rich to tell them of his decision and to explain it. He was going to take a bit of time off, but no doubt their paths would cross as he would be seeking similar work before too long. To Rich he said, "Do not gloat about this, because I can soon be replaced. It will not change his mind about what he will do. He is not finished with this business yet. Rich, stay sharp." To Dean he said, "Keep him away from that funeral. I do not know how you and Rich, or Rich and your dad, are going to come out of this, but I do know if he tries to make a spectacle at the funeral it will be much harder."

CHAPTER 28.

"You and I will meet again, When we're least expecting it, One day in some far off place, I will recognize your face, I won't say goodbye my friend, For you and I will meet again." - Tom Petty.

Tommy got all the fighters together ahead of the crematorium service.
"No-one should feel bad if they need to shed a tear or openly cry. A funeral service is a time to feel sorrow, to mourn the passing of someone close to you. It's when you descend to your lowest ebb, so you can then begin to peel that layer of sadness away and gradually move on with your life. Today, is about saying good-bye to our PD...." The lump in his throat at the mention of PD, caused him to pause, break away from all the eyes seeking his, breathe in deeply and blow it out with force. He looked at the faces in front of him, "Just bear with me a second...." A quiver in his voice, he ended with,
"Boxers can feel pain too, do not be ashamed. We all know what physical pain is, but this is different. This is not done to you, it comes from within. I can't say I understand it, but what I do understand is that no matter how much you battle with it, it is going to do its thing. This is not the pain of losing, this is the pain of a loss and we have lost a powerful force in all our lives. Like all of you I am angry at how he was taken, I am mad that the person who did this has not been caught and I am beyond pissed that I didn't get to say good-bye or thank you to him. Most of all I am hurting. I am told that will ease with time and I hope so, because right now it feels almost unbearable. But, I will bear it, and we will bear it, because PD would expect that of us. PD knows today is a day, where something other than the walls of his gym can cry."

The funeral was horrible, simply horrible. The crematorium was packed with those who had trained at the gym and the ages ranged from teenagers to those in their forties. Every seat was taken and plenty more were happy to stand to be part of the service. PD was a much loved individual.

Donna asked to do a reading;

"Like many of you here today, I spent much of my time in a cramped, little fighting gym, where a silly old man, in a ridiculous, frayed beanie hat, used to hold court. He pushed us to be the best we can, he goaded us to work harder when we needed it and he taught us how to be boxers. He thought he could dance, but actually he merely waved his arms to his slouching shuffle. He thought his jokes were funny, but Peter Kay has little to worry about. He thought he could sing, but who knows how they were meant to sound as the songs were so old. I think only he knew them. I'm guessing not how he sang them and I wish he had learned a few different lines to those same few over and over.

However, look around you today at the people who have come to pay their respects and there is no doubt; this was a special man." She caught herself as the emotion of the occasion unveiled itself. The tears were running down her face and she gulped a couple of times in an attempt to control her cracking voice. "Sorry," she looked away and wiped her tears.

"In the blink of an eye, this community has lost a great servant and, to me at least, a great man. A needless piece of violence and so many of us have to deal with a void in our lives that can never be replaced. I am sure the gym will carry on, but I am not sure when, if ever, I will walk through that door and not expect to see PD grinning at me. I hope never, because then he lives on. Let me end with one of his sayings, slightly changed for today."

"It might not be the law of the land, but for me PD rules. Thanks for the ride, for you we will make sure it continues."

She looked at the coffin and though it took considerable effort to speak without losing total control, she said, "PD, I love you." Then she retook her seat. The coffin was withdrawn to the strains of the song he most liked to sing;

'Sing, Muhammed, Muhammed Ali.
He floats like a butterfly and stings like a bee.
Muhammed, the black superman.
Who calls to the other guy I'm Ali catch me if you can'.

* * *

Dean had managed to talk Russ out of attending, but it was not easy as this was exactly the kind of attention the old man craved. Doing something out of the ordinary, unexpected, then people talked, and his job was so much easier. He had tried to pull on his heart strings about Rich and their relationship going forward, but Russ was having none of it; he was the dad and it was up to Rich to make the peace. So, he went for the one thing he knew would resonate with Russ; his image. Would attending the funeral of a man he had issued the contact on, just to rub some noses in it, add to his credibility or might he lose some respect? It was as if he had pushed the button on a slot machine and come up with three jackpot signs. The cogs were whirring as Russ heard the words 'lose respect'. Maybe Dean was right. Plenty of time to conclude his business with Donna, so leave it alone at the funeral.

Anyway, he was still furious at those incompetent pair of idiots who had killed PD.

How simple could it have been? Give him a scare and a message for Donna. Say Russ was still waiting for a name and until he got it no-one she knew was safe. Punch him in the balls or the gut and then give him a kicking, making sure there would be plenty of bruises on show. Then, perhaps, this gobby cow would do as she was told. But no, they thought a smack to the back of his head with a heavy dumbbell was a better idea. Surprise, surprise, they bloody well killed him straight out.

He paid them off the next day with Chan in attendance and made it quite clear not to come back to this neighbourhood. If they did, Chan was under instruction to bury them.

CHAPTER 29.

"Children learn more from what you are than what you teach." – W E B DuBois.

It's two days after the funeral and Donna wants everything back to normal or at least as normal as they can be. She moved back into her flat and has resumed her shifts at work. The manager has been great in covering for her, knowing how close she and PD were, but sitting around and just thinking is not such a brilliant idea. With all she still had going on, keeping busy was the best policy.

As she left off from the supermarket and began the walk home, a large, silver Audi car pulled up alongside her.
"You Donna?"
"Who are you?"
"We couldn't make the funeral the other day, so we wondered how it went. That's all."

She couldn't remember seeing these two at the gym, although she could not really make out the one on the far side of the car. The mention of PD threw her off guard and she loosened up a little.

"It went OK for a funeral. How did you know PD?"
"Well, we didn't, but our boss did. Mr. Tomkins." She bristled. In light of what had happened to PD perhaps she should be scared right now, but anger was her overriding emotion.
"Now before you say or do anything silly, we have something to show you." The guy nearest then held up a picture of Layla, then Maggie and finally Sam.
"Do we have your attention?" She nodded. The back window of the car whirred as the motor took the glass down to half way and stopped. Then Rav appeared. She had not realised anyone was in the back. He spoke;

"There's a good girl. Mr. Tomkins is still waiting for a name from you and he is getting impatient. I owe you bitch, so please don't hurry to provide that name as I am enjoying this." With that the car sped off. She was shaken. They had pictures of the kids and Layla and if they could kill PD, why not them too?

She called her dad first, then Layla and then Rich. Dog was to stay close to Maggie and Sam. Layla was to stay close to Dog. From Rich she wanted to know if Russ could, and would, hurt an innocent woman and kids. "Yes. I would say he is capable of anything. I have never known him to put a hit on anyone like that, but I cannot say he hasn't or won't." All three were summoned to be at Donna's that evening.

* * *

Rich came after the kids were in bed; they had enough going on with the arrival on the scene of a grandad, without a boyfriend appearing too. Even though she had already spoken to each of them, Donna went through the altercation earlier that afternoon and how she did not know what to do. The death of PD and the torrent of mental suffering it had caused, was hampering her ability to think straight, so she needed help.

"What I do know is that I cannot give Russ a name for him to go and beat the crap out of. He will not accept mine, he has taken PD away from me as a warning and this afternoon made it clear he isn't done yet. What do I do?"

Rich spoke, "Chan called me earlier to say he's had enough and he no longer works for my dad. That's good, in that the best minder I know of is no longer protecting dad. That might just make him think. However, it might not. The downside is, rather than a true pro at what he does, we are now having to deal with cowboys, and dangerous ones at that."
"It's time for me to speak to Russ." Dog was calm and controlled. "Whether I agreed with how you wanted things to pan out does not matter as we are where we are. That said, it is time to fight back."
"Rich, what do you think?"
"You mean, do I think your dad should go after mine? Obviously no! I do not like that."
"So, what should we do then?"
"Get away from here. Let's you, me and the kids leave tonight."
"What about dad? What about Layla? Nope, I get why you are saying that, but we cannot risk him taking it out on those we leave behind."
"Layla?"
"I am scared shitless, so no point in asking me. I just want this over."
"OK, dad you can meet with Russ, but listen to me. I want to find out if Rich and me can make it through all this, because I think I love him, so if you disfigure his father, we will have one more massive obstacle to overcome. Talk. Scare him. But do not, DO NOT, injure or god forbid kill him. Have you heard me?"
"I will try to control myself," he winked at Rich. "No point wasting time, I'm going tonight."

As Dog readied himself to leave and Layla left the room to 'watch some rubbish telly to keep me sane', Rich spoke to Donna. "I love you too, you do know that?" He gently took her hand and they interlocked their fingers. She laid the flat of her palm on his chest, "Listen, it is very clear that we have feelings for each other, but we have to take things ultra-slow for the time being. What we do will affect so many other people. Could you really live without Russ in your life? What about if he makes Dean choose between him and you? Christ Rich, are we just heaping more pain in when neither of us really knows if you and me has legs?" He held both her hands, more tightly this time and looked straight at her.

"I have decided to jack the business in. It's weird that in such a short space of time I have gone from thinking this was my life for ever and ever, to seeing that it is not for me. Perhaps my dad was like me when he was my age, but look at him now. I still love him, but I no longer want to be, him. I have no idea what I will do, but I do know that life is not for me."
"Have you told him?"
"No. I am going to speak to Dean first and then tell him."
"Are you sure? He is not going to like it and they are your family. What about if he will not have anything to do with you? It's a massive decision Rich, because if we don't make it as a couple he will not let you back in easily."
"If he won't accept my decision and refuses to have anything to do with me, then we both lose. Orders or not, Dean will keep in touch, I can guarantee that. I'm not sure you're listening. My involvement with you has opened up my senses to the life I was leading, but even if we call it off I will still not want that life anymore. It demands business comes ahead of everything, including family. It has made my dad a bitter, uncaring man, driven by power and money. He loved my mother, she hated the business. He chose the business over mum. The way I feel right now, that is not a choice I could make. Telling him I am out, is me showing that." She hugged him.
"You are too soppy to be a thug anyway."
"Yeah, that is something else I have realised."

CHAPTER 30.

If you want to enter hell, don't complain of the dark; you can't blame the world for being unfair if you start on the path of the rebel. – Liu Xiaobo.

Russ was attending a charity auction and was heading straight there from work, so he decided to tidy up some paperwork to fill the time up to when he had to leave. The only way the business could continue as it did was if he had legitimate ways of making money, to help with laundering dirty cash and to obscure the view of the other income streams. That meant he had to deal with bills, tax, unhappy tenants and all the rest of the crap that goes with heading up an organisation like his. Carly and Rav did all the donkey work, but he still liked to know about all the detail. That incurred him in using his time to read and sign all those pieces of paper or sign off e-mails etc. He was just about to get changed into his tuxedo, when the door to his office burst open, crashing against its hinges and flying back towards the frame where a rough hand stopped it in its track.

"What the fuc......."

"Evening Russ." Dog entered and in contrast to his entrance, calmly and purposefully closed the door behind him. "So, I understand you are a danger-Russ man. You do not look too dangerous to me."

Russ knew of Dog, but with the shock of his arrival it took him a couple of seconds to recognise him.

"Ahhh. Daddy to the rescue is it? With what I can call on, please don't think I am being rude if I say you on your tod doesn't have me shaking in my boots."

"You arrogant twat. You have no idea what I can 'call on' and before you get too cock sure, look around you.................. just me and you. Perhaps, I should beat the crap out of you here and now."

"You won't do that."

"Won't I now? What makes you so sure?"

"I have survived many a threat over the years and look, I am still here. With age comes wisdom and, in my case, also a handgun." He produced a black pistol and pointed it at Dog. "This, is what makes me so sure."

"Is that meant to scare me? It doesn't. Put it down as I am only here to talk tonight, unless you intend to use that. Once you have heard me out I am sure you will realise that would be bad for your health."

"You mean, YOUR health?"

"I said what I meant. Now put it down and let us see if we can come to an accord,

before we tear lumps out of each other and our families. PUT IT DOWN." Russ did not move for several seconds, then laid it down on his desk, easily within reach should he need it.
"What exactly do we have to talk about that I will find of any interest?"
"You and yours, have involved my daughter in your sleazy little world and I want you to stop whatever it is you have planned. I have grandchildren to consider, so I am asking you nicely."
"You taking the piss? Fuck off."
"If I had my way you would have been a mangled inpatient a while ago, but Donna thought there was a better way. I said I was asking nicely as that's what she wanted me to do; she is a decent person unlike you and me. As that does not seem to have been looked upon too favourably, I will do things my way." His eyes stared with a chilling intent and his face went taut. It was a look Russ knew very well as he had seen so many people rage at him. Dog did not move one muscle; he just looked at Russ.
"PD is dead. He should not be. Bad mistake and poor control, Russy boy. Chan has stopped providing the shield you relied on to keep order for so long and now you have amateurs around you. Rich, your blood, is having to choose between you and the business, or Donna. Man, you are fucked up."
"Shit happens. PD was a freak accident. Chan can be replaced and has been. Rich is fuck all to do with you. You have 2 minutes to get to the point."
"Freak accidents happen when you employ wastes of space and if you think those two goons outside can replace Chan, you had better think again."
"They know what to do."
"You sure about that? I introduced myself a while ago. Why not call them to come and scare me off?"
"I don't need them to get rid of you as I have my good friend here, remember? Get to the point, you're boring me."
Dog reached in his pocket and threw two mobile phones on the desk.
"I 'somehow' managed to sneak up on these 'professionals' of yours and put a blade to the bigger one's throat. Then I showed them a corkscrew and some nutcrackers and made it clear what I would do with them if they EVER pissed me off. When they heard who I was, they seemed really compliant. Funny that. I said I would return their phones to you. They're gone for good I'd guess."
Russ felt the hair on his neck stand upright.
"We both know I can keep on recruiting, no big deal."
"We both know I can keep scaring them off and in true Russ Tomkins style, next time I might use those nutcrackers to help deter future recruits."
Russ picked up the gun.
"Time you went."
"You seem to think this gun frightens me, so let's clear that up. I made a number of close associates, whilst at her majesty's pleasure, and these are men you do not want to upset, if you know what I mean. On your head Russ, is a living contract. If I die of anything at all suspicious, so will you. I think they may consider a gunshot to be a

little bit suspicious, don't you? I mean, hardly natural causes, is it? Now perhaps you get why that pea shooter is not overly intimidating. Use it on me, and you die."
"I am not that easy to get at, so perhaps I will put one in you and then take my chances."
"Not that easy! Look across the desk Russ. Anyway, do it. I will be dead and I'm honest enough to know my passing will not cause a ripple in many people's lives. But, and it's a big but, you will be dead too very soon after and seriously, who will care? You are doing your absolute best to fuck it up with your sons and that is all you have got. With you out of the way they will have all their time taken up with fighting off the pretenders to the throne. Chances are the pack will overrun them."
"Time's up."
"Point is Russ, old boy, did you realise time is up, but it's for you. I will continue to scare off any muscle you hire, and I will make my acquaintance with your other son too; Dean, isn't it? I am untouchable by you, so who knows what other mischief I can cause to your world? You call time on this stupid vendetta against Donna, and I mean now, or we will meet up again soon. Night Russ."
Dog backed away and was gone. Russ was motionless as he processed all that had been said. His head was pounding. He dialled a number and said, "I need two guys down here tonight and make sure they don't scare easy.........yeah, everything's fine......no, that's all. Thanks." He put his mobile down and stared at his desk, going over and over what had been said. Then he rose and in the same rapid motion threw one mobile against the wall and then the other. If it was meant to make him feel better, it didn't.

He had been looking forward to the charity auction, but there was no way he was going now as he had to get his head right and think what to do next. He had faced difficult situations like this many times over the years, but somehow this felt different. Why? He was racking his brains, because it was clouding his thought process. Had he never faced a foe like Dog? Rubbish. He had seen off some of the most ruthless adversaries anyone would come across and swatted them away without a second thought. What that bastard said, had got under his skin though. Honestly, this fucking business had cost him Chan, caused friction with Rich, no doubt given him high blood pressure and he was having to come to terms with knowing his life was in peril, if he did what his gut told him to do. Sure, there was always a target on his back, but this time it felt closer, the threat ever more real. Face it Russ, you're getting old and mortality is becoming more precious with age.

He reached into the bottom drawer, pulled out a bottle of Glengoyne single malt whisky, along with his personalised lead crystal tumbler. It was engraved with *Danger Dad* and had been a present from Rich and Dean some time ago. He poured a small slug and then sniffed the aroma, before sipping at it neat. He held the glass in one hand, swirled the liquid as he tipped back his seat and enjoyed the heat as it descended down his throat. Some people said whisky was brown, but to him it was golden. He allowed himself a few minutes to get lost in the waves he was making in the glass. Enjoy these few minutes of tranquility shutting out all the crap going on and when ready, get those thoughts back under control.

CHAPTER 31.

"Friendship is like a walk in the wood; you may not know the terrain too well or even know where you are headed yet you enjoy it all the same!" — Jaachynma N.E. Agu.

Rich called Dean and said he wanted to meet up as he had something to discuss with him.
"You too?"
"What do you mean?"
"Dad's just been on and wants me in to see him before lunch."
"I need to see you before him, so how about we meet in an hour at The Park and you can treat me to breakfast?"
"What's going on Rich? I'm in the dark about what is happening to cause all this activity?"
"I will tell you over the bacon butty and coffee."

* * *

The Park was a club the firm had a controlling interest in and it was not only a good earner, but also mostly legit. Russ did not mind a bit of pill supplying going on, as long as the provider had paid for his 'pitch' and every so often a bit of dirty money might be given a spring clean when Rav worked it through the books. It was quiet in the mornings, with only a few employees in, cleaning up or getting ready for later, so the boys often met for a mid-morning break there and always persuaded someone to rustle them up a bite and cuppa. They sat at one of the tables in the centre of the room as always, because this was far enough away from everyone to be out of earshot.

"Right Rich, come on, tell me what's going on?"
"I have decided to get out of the business."
"Do what?"
"You heard me. I want to chat to you before I tell dad, although I think he has got an inkling already. He told me I had to choose; in or out and all that goes with it."
"What do you intend to do if you're not part of the firm?"

"No idea."

"Rich, this is your brother speaking; is she worth it?"

"Yes, absolutely. Remember, we found her. Perhaps it's just meant to be. We have had such an easy life and then I find something that is going to be so hard to make a go of, and yet, I can't get enough of it. That life was an existence. Now, I'm alive and living."

"Wow."

"But, it's not just Donna. We grew into this way of life and yes, the money is really good and all that goes with it. But, I have seen what we do to people, and being on the other side has really made me think. Plus, dad will always do what is right for the business over what is right for us, that's his way and he is proud of it. I have now met someone who does not think like that. Family comes above everything else. Dean, I have to tell you it is something special to see. If I carry on as we are, then at some point I might need to act like dad. What about if I have a wife and kids by then? Either I give them up or someone, like us, can use them against me."

"Jeez, you have got it bad."

"I'm not asking you to understand or agree with me, but I would like you to make sure we stay in contact. I think dad may want me disowned. You are my best mate, as well as my brother, and through this fucking business of dad's I have lost my mother and quite possibly now my dad. He won't let us contact mum and we both know I will not be welcome when I go through with this. The choice will be clear Dean; freeze me out or we meet without him knowing and you suffer the grief if he finds out."

"Shit Rich, dad wouldn't do that."

"No? Then come with me now and I will tell him in front of you. Let's see who is right."

Rich downed the remnants of his coffee and stood up.

"Chan made sure dad didn't go too far before, because he doesn't see me as his son when his temper takes over. I will stand up for myself, but Dean, you might need to step in if it looks like he is doing me permanent damage. Got it?"

"Shut the fuck up. He is our dad, he's not capable of anything like that towards us."

"Whatever. Just be ready."

* * *

Russ had not expected both his sons, just Dean, so he was a bit taken back when they showed up together. He was good at reading people and something was not right about their body language as they walked in. Dean's head was down, avoiding eye contact. Rich looked scared. Yeah, scared. He swooped back in his chair and up went the steeple of fingers.

"I asked Dean here to discuss some business stuff, so I assume you're here for that too?"
"No dad."
"What then?"
He swallowed, looked at the floor and then at his dad.
"You told me I had to decide about whether this business is right for me and I have. It isn't. I cannot be you, dad."
"What is so wrong with me then? I can't remember you whinging about me when you were driving around in your beamer and flashing the cash. All of a sudden, this bird comes along and now I'm a bad person, is that it? Can't you see she has turned you against me?"
"I hope me and Donna are in for the long haul, but if we go our separate ways tomorrow, I will still want out."
"Oh, will you now?"
"Yes. It is the life you wanted, but it is no longer what I want and stuff the cars and cash...."
"Easy to say, but what about when you live in some dive and struggle to make ends meet?"
"I don't know until it happens, BUT I will sleep OK at night and that is more than I will if I stick with the firm."
"I've heard enough. Your wish is granted, you are out. No more handouts from me though. In fact, let us avoid each other from now on as I don't know if I will always be able to contain my anger if I see you. I hope you don't think this means I'm done with that little bitch of yours either. Tell her to stay vigilant, my boy."
Rich did not know whether to move and actually he was not sure if he was physically capable as the threat and intensity from his dad were debilitating for him. Russ looked at Dean,
"Same for you Dean, no contact with him. Time for us decide what to do with his gobby girlfriend now."
"Dad, Rich said you would want him completely out of your life and I said you wouldn't. This whole affair is not worth me losing my brother over and it should not be worth you losing such a terrific son either."
"Not you as well Dean."
"No, not me too. I want to stay in the business, but I will not disown or not speak to Rich. Full stop. You have chosen how to live your life, but you cannot impose that on me."
"Then perhaps you are not up to what it takes."
"Perhaps. That means you either carry on forever, you get someone other than blood to run it for you or, you accept I do it my way as and when that time comes."
Russ was visibly stunned. On top of everything else, now Rich wanted out and Dean was standing up to him.
"Get out, I need to think." As Dean looked to speak again, Russ broke eye contact, turned his head very deliberately away from him and pointed at the door. "Get out."

They left. Russ was now alone with his thoughts. Who could have known that one petty little piece of business could cause all this aggravation? Think man, think. It was so much to consider. Normally, he knew the end goal was to make money or maintain his reputation and that was simple. This was anything but.

After much head scratching and getting nowhere, he reached for the Glengoyne. Bit early in the day, but he needed to slow the cyclone in his head down a bit as it kept sucking one thought in and then throwing another one out. He could not get his mind composed, so time for a little golden assistance to pacify him. He needed a distraction and then he would return to this later. It was far too important to rush things and if Russ knew anything, it was that his hothead was not a great tool for coming to reasoned outcomes.

"Carly," he buzzed through to reception, "Can you come in here please?" She arrived within a minute, poking her head around his door. "Is everything OK Mr. Tomkins?" He waved her in and pointed at the chair on the other side of his desk for her to sit on, "Of course." She noticed the tumbler on his desk and he clocked her looking at it. "I have only had a snifter and I won't be making a habit of drinking this early." He leant back.
"Tell me Carly, what is going on in your life?"
"Sorry?"
"I'm interested. What is the most important thing happening in your world right now."
She looked puzzled. Russ was always pleasant to her, but to engage in conversation, that had never happened before. Just how much drink had he got through? She sat upright in the chair.
"Well, me and my boyfriend are looking at moving in together and trying to find a place."
"Have I met him?"
"Uh.... no."
"Why not?"
"He's....... scared of you!"
Russ liked her honesty and he really liked the reason. He roared out a guffaw.
"Then he is a wise young man. How about if I sorted you out a place to rent off me?"
He saw a rabbit in the headlights in front of him and obviously his facial expression gave away that he had seen it.
"Thank you Mr. Tomkins, that's very kind, but.......... if you do not mind we will arrange it so there is no conflict between work and my personal life." What a great answer thought Russ, maybe he could make better use of his receptionist as she clearly had a brain on her.
"Smart girl. Do you like working here Carly?"
"Yes, of course."
"Why?" straight questions were the best way to understand people he had found, and it helped him recognise any untruths.

"Why?" she echoed back at him.

"Yes. Why do you like working here?" He sat forward, probably a reflex from when he needed to put the squeeze on the poor sod sat in front of him in different type meetings, but it had the desired effect on Carly as she spoke up.

"You pay well for what I do, it's not that difficult for me and apart from the days when you're stressed, you are nice to work for."

"How often am I 'stressed'?"

"Don't know, it varies. Of late, quite a bit of the time."

"Yeah, lots going on at the minute. Sorry." It was her turn to leak surprise. Did he just say sorry? She felt an uncomfortable gap in the conversation and filled it.

"Not having Chan around or seeing as much of Rich is a shame, because I like both of them." He said nothing for a while, but just sank back into the comfort of his chair.

"Yeah. Thanks Carly, you have been a terrific help. I hope you and the boyfriend find somewhere soon." She gave a small nod of her head, smiled nicely and still with a bemused look, left him. Russ sat for a few minutes, staring out of his window and then turned to put the top back on the bottle, before filing it back in the drawer.

This was a simple decision to make.

"Carly." He buzzed her again.

"Yes Mr. Tomkins."

"Would you like to learn about bookkeeping? I was wondering about getting Rav to show you the ropes."

"That would be really good. Thank you, Mr. Tomkins."

"I will speak to Rav and you get started on finding a new receptionist please. That OK?"

"Urm, yes." He put the phone down and smiled. Carly could learn the books, he would let her get proficient and then have it out with Rav.

That little shit could pay up and go or stay and be in his pocket big time.

An extra receptionist salary was not going to hurt him, so it was a good plan. He smiled. That was the easy one done with, now to get back to the main order of the day; the future of the firm. His look could be mistaken for displeasure, but he was concentrating hard.

CHAPTER 32.

"Do not mistake my kindness for weakness. I am kind to everyone, but when someone is unkind to me, weak is not what you are going to remember about me."
—Al Capone.

Stoney was a long established, but local bookie, who had his fingers in most local sporting activities. He had done well for himself. He looked like a Rottweiler in a top end dog coat when he got suited up. His large, round, black face, that had not been short of a few beatings, contrasted with his Hugo Boss, virgin wool, two piece in Natural.

His uncompromising style meant you knew better than to not pay up when he came calling and if he had to return, he rarely came alone. His own days of handing out beatings were long gone, as he paid others to do that now, so his frame was more fat than muscle nowadays. Age was taking its toll too, which meant he was not the mean machine he once was. Tablets helped keep his heart healthy and anything that affected his blood pressure was to be avoided. Overweight and teetering on poor health or not, on the streets he was respected. He considered himself a success.

Stoney did not like it one little bit that those lads of Russ had tried to fit him up. The drums had been beating loudly since that night, so he soon found out what had been planned. Mind you, he had pretty much worked it out anyway from how Russ had reacted. Then, to rub salt in, he had been told one of them was servicing his missus. She denied it, but little clues like the new lingerie, sudden loss of weight and more interest in how she looked, were perhaps signs she was getting hers somewhere else. He was not happy, but what could he do? He spoke to a few mates and aired his grievances, but he was against the might of Russ. As a bookie he knew which fights were worth a punt and which ones were definitely not. He could have been seriously out of pocket and that was not right, so he told a few more people about what had gone on. They listened, some empathised, but all warned him to tread carefully.

After another row with his wife, she had stormed out earlier and was not coming back for a few days. He was fed up that she was not at all interested in his advances and he accused her of looking after some young beef. This time she had not denied it, she had merely taken him to task on how he had let himself go. Both said some cruel things. He would give it a day or so and make contact. If she gave up this new buck, he would take her back and promise to lose a few pounds or join a gym or whatever.

The doorbell rang. There was Russ.
"House visits Russ, what's up?"
"Evening Stoney. Am I coming in or what?"
He stood aside, wary, but as welcoming as he could be. They went into the kitchen.
"Where's the missus?"
"Out for the night, getting pissed somewhere."
"Good."
"Drink Russ?"
"No thanks. Not a social call. You've been bad mouthing me, Stoney."
Him and Russ went back a long way and he knew this was not good news. Calling on him at home and straight to the point, shit this was serious.
"Not exactly what you would call bad mouthing. Am I happy I got set up by your boys? No. Would you be?"
"I live in the penthouse of our universe Stoney, so when I get unhappy everyone in the floors below me had better watch out. You live on the middle floors; the people who live above you could not give a shit if you are unhappy."
"It's not right Russ, you know that."
"Neither is this."
His speed was too much for Stoney as he grabbed a kitchen knife and lunged. Self preservation took over and Stoney moved backwards and away from Russ, only to be blocked by the large cabinet doors. A knee from Russ to the lower abdomen took all the wind out of Stoney. His hand was wrenched upwards and pinned to the wooden door. The knife was lifted up high and ferociously brought down to penetrate his palm and pierce the oak panel. It was deep enough to be secure. The pain took a second to register and then he let out a muffled howl. Instinct told him to remove the knife, but Russ slapped his other hand away. "Touch it and I will crucify you."

Stoney was finding it hard to breathe as the pain intensified and he was vulnerable to whatever Russ had planned. He knew what this man was capable of and to be anything other than afraid would be stupid. He was terrified, gasping for air and saliva was blown out of his mouth with every desperate pant.
"What the fuck Russ!"
"You know the order of things. What did you think was going to happen? Did it really ever cross your mind I might turn a deaf ear, because we've known each other for so long? That would show weakness and unfortunately for you, I need everyone on my streets to know there is no weakness. I am still who you all answer to. You are going to have to pay for thinking you could take liberties with me. Then you had better tell all those same people you have been mouthing off to, that Russ Tomkins does not react well to having the piss taken. If not, I will return and separate your hand from your arm."
"Russ, no."

"If you don't hold your weight off that hand the pain will be intense as the knife slices you. Who knows what permanent damage you might do. However, I am going to make it difficult for you to stand up straight...." With that he kicked Stoney in the knee with as much force as he could manage. Stoney slumped down as the excruciating pain caused surges of hot and cold to rush through him. Then, as the knife went to work, he felt nauseous. He spat out more spittle, breathed really deeply and did his best to support himself on his good leg. He lent against the cabinet door and looked at Russ.
"This is wrong!" his voice was loud, "All because of bad timing, is that it? Whatever is going on with you, do not take it out on me. Please, I beg you. We go back so far, and I don't deserve this, just because you want to show who is the boss." He finished and banged his head back connecting with the wood.
Russ propped himself up on a bar stool next to the breakfast bar and looked at Stoney. He was helpless. Blood pouring out of his hand, a seriously damaged knee and look at him, old, obese and pathetic. He lifted himself up and headed for Stoney, who pushed an arm out to keep him away, but Russ easily evaded it and grabbed the knife. Stoney gasped and grabbed Russ on the shoulder expecting the worst, but Russ simply pulled the knife out and watched as his beaten prey slid down onto the floor grabbing at his hand. Russ flew the knife across the floor.
"Make sure those who need to know hear about this." Then he walked out.

Stoney waited for him to leave and heard the front door close. Then he let his head rest on the floor. The cocktail of extreme fear, intense pain, and enormous relief was too much for him. He cried. He had not done that since he was a young lad. Tonight, had shaken him deep to his very core. He sniffed and using his head and elbow as levers, straightened himself into a sitting position. He grabbed a tea towel and wrapped his hand in it, wincing at the pain with every coil. Using his good arm and leg and other parts of his body that were still functioning, he delicately got himself into a position where he could drag his body across the kitchen floor. Reaching up, he grabbed his mobile phone. He vigorously blew out through his mouth, shook his head, as if trying to jerk something off it, and closed his eyes as he focused on what he needed to do. It kind of worked, as he felt his voice was reasonably steady. Then he dialled;
"Love? I need you to come home tonight............. because Russ has been round......yes, I'm OK, but I could do with a plaster or two..................." The intake of breath and high-pitched noises coming from the other end were clear evidence she knew what that meant. "........ yeah, OK.................don't be long, eh."

CHAPTER 33.

"The surest cure for vanity is loneliness." - Tom Wolfe.

Rich delayed getting to the flat until he knew Donna would be back from taking the kids to school and then made his way to her front door. He knocked, and she greeted him with a smile, kiss and quick hug. His response was not what she would call passionate and he had a look that said he was carrying a heavy weight with him. She pulled him in and closed the door.
"What's up, you seem distant?"
"Well, I don't know what this means, but apparently dad wants to see you, me and your dad, along with my brother, at his office later this morning. Dean phoned me an hour ago."
"He does know we have a life and other things to do, does he?"
"Donna! Who cares? This sounds serious. Where's your dad?"
"Right here." Dog was standing in the kitchen doorway and had clearly heard them speaking. No-one said anything for a while, then Rich gave in as he could not stand the silence anymore.
"So? What do you think this means?"
"I have no intention of wasting any time or effort even thinking about that," Dog was calm, and he hoped his voice would have a calming effect on everyone else. "If Donna wants to go, we find out then. Donna?"
"Whatever he wants to tell us we are going to find out one way or another, so let's bite the bullet and go see what this is about. He likes a drama your old man, doesn't he? I will make sure Layla can collect the kids if needs be and then let's go; otherwise we sit around and just think and wind ourselves up even more." Dog raised one eyebrow.
"OK, Rich and me, wind ourselves up. Happy now?" he grinned and tilted his head as approval for her acknowledging his point.

* * *

They piled into the black BMW. Rich reminded himself the car was just one perk he might have to give up very soon. He loved this piece of German technological wizardry as he hardly had to think to drive it. The ride itself was sublime. It impressed his mates, more important it had impressed the birds and he felt great every time he drove it. Donna reached over and squeezed his arm; it's almost as if she can read my mind, he thought, but she was not concerned with big boy toys. Her concerns were on a more mature level.

Russ was used to summoning people to him and knew full well they would be shitting themselves thinking about what he wanted. He was like a cat who is not content to just kill some poor mouse or bird, they have to play with it first. He messed with your head and gained pleasure from doing so. "Rich, I think I hate your dad." Rich beamed, "I'm sure he will be delighted to hear that. He has more enemies than friends and every new hater only tells him he is doing his job right." She pushed his arm as she let go and crossed hers in front of her chest. "It's true and you know it. Not sure what good sulking will do and it's not my fault how he is." She was looking out of her window and without turning her head at all she said,
"I am not sulking, and IT IS YOUR FAULT I found out how he is."
"Feel better now?"
"Much."
"Thought so." Then they fell silent, a typical car journey for squabbling couples everywhere.

Dog sniggered to himself when they arrived as he spotted some new faces on duty for Russ, either lurking about inconspicuously or sitting in large saloon cars. I might well be meeting you very soon, he thought, as his brain registered each one. They got out of the car and Rich led the way with Donna close behind. He reached back for her hand and she clasped hold of it and gripped it tightly. Dog was a few paces back, taking everything in. He did not do fear, he did anticipation.

Carly looked up as they arrived and was a little surprised as Rich marched through the reception area and disappeared, dragging Donna with him. She gave her a brief smile. Carly reciprocated. Then Dog ambled in behind and followed them. He looked at Carly and simply said, "I'm with them," and was gone. She was used to some tough men visiting Russ, but this one looked as bad as any of them. Whether he was with them or not, she was hardly likely to stop him.

She picked up the phone, "Mr. Tomki........." he cut her short, "I know Carly, Rich is in here already. I was expecting him, just a bit later. Tell Dean to get in sharpish as soon as he arrives please." Russ put the receiver down. He steepled his fingers and lent back, "Sit down then. We do nothing until Dean gets here." Rich did as he was told, and Donna grabbed the seat next to him. Dog was less comfortable in sitting down as the chairs had their backs to the door and that made him nervous. Russ knew instantly what he was thinking. Kindred spirits. "If I was going to have you popped I would hardly choose my own office having called you to a meeting, would I? However, move the chair to where you will be comfortable if that helps." Dog lifted the chair and placed it against a wall. He sat down, "Now I'm happy..........er!" He slouched down and looked round the office.

Dean barged through the door within a few minutes, making one heck of an entrance as he clearly thought he was late. It was a good job he did arrive then as the uncomfortable silence was beyond a joke. He lent against a wall near Rich and tried to look cool and collected. It was a look he might need some more practice at as he was feeling anything but calm and his acting was rubbish. Russ interlocked the bottom three fingers of his hands. Still steepled, he pressed his index fingers to his nose as he pursed his lips. He was being very deliberate about what he would say, and he was also making sure he had everyone's attention. He had read about famous politician's, who made a point of keeping a period of silence between the audience stopping clapping and them, start speaking. It made the crowd listen more intently. There might not be any clapping, but the effect was what he was after. He wanted their minds to be only thinking about him and what he had to say. Just to be sure, he went for his show stopper.

Russ reached into his top drawer and pulled out his handgun, resting it just in front of him. Then he looked at each of them in turn. Dean, hands behind his back, left leg over right, acting tough, but every few seconds the hands pushed him slightly away from the wall and then he fell back again. It gave his nerves away. Rich and Donna had swapped glances and then were in a fast loop of looking at the gun, then at him, gun, him. Dog was motionless. He was the first to speak.
"I thought we had established that even if you did use that gun it would only end up with you getting yours."
"No. We established that if I used it on YOU, I would get whacked. We never mentioned her." With that he lifted the gun and pointed it at Donna. My God, he has got me here to kill me. She began involuntarily shaking. Rich saw it and squeezed her hand.
"Do I have your attention now Dog?"
"You know I will kill you if you do anything to her."
"I do know that....... but, she will still be DEAD." He made a point of emphasising this last word in both volume and expression. His experience was, if people thought they, or someone they cared about, might be in danger of getting killed, they could block it out, if not fully, at least partially. Hearing it was far more real, more effective at influencing them to do what they needed to. Being loud and pointed always hit the mark.
"There was a danger of you coming in here today and thinking you had all the power and that I was running scared. Well, let us put that right. I have the power, because I have the gun." He looked at Dog. "Last time of asking; do I have your attention now?" Dog paused.
"Dad!" Donna screamed.
"OK, OK. You have my attention."
"Good." He put the gun down on the desk, but did not lose an ounce of the intensity

as his eyes burned into Dog. "Now leave and then the rest of us can continue."
"I am going nowhere. Donna needs me......," Russ lifted the gun up and aimed it at Donna, but this time he did so quickly and stood up at the same time. It was dramatic, it was scary, and it served its purpose. "Get the fuck out so we can carry on or she dies." Dog held his hands up in half submission and began to move towards the door. "You might think this is a time to say something clever, tough or reassuring to your daughter, but it is not. Just get out; now!" The gun was starting to shake a little in his hand, but his voice had not deviated from its firm, tenacious tone. Dog left, his body language showing defeat, but also fury. His shoulders were partially slumped, but his fists were tight little clenched balls; weapons he could not use right now. Russ waited a few seconds and then picked up his phone. "Carly, has that tough looking man left yet?.....Good. Thank you." He replaced the handset in its holder. Without looking at anyone, he put the gun away in its drawer and sat down.

"There was a problem with your dad staying that would have not fitted well with what I am about to say. He paid a visit to me recently, right here, and I worry that he will think it is entirely because of that I have made the decisions I have. It is not. He cannot protect you from me. He will not be able to accept that. There is only space for one alpha male in a room, and anytime I am around, it is me. He would have trouble with that. These two know it's me and you do not care as all that macho stuff is no doubt beyond you. Before I state the main purpose of this little get together, let me say that if he ever threatens me again, I will have him killed." He did not spill a drop of emotion as he said this. Killing was not alien to him and there was to be no doubt, he meant what he said. It was almost unnerving, how he could discuss the taking of a life in such a cold way, but it only served to underline the validity of his statement.

"I have quite a bit to say and I want you all to listen really well. We can discuss it afterwards, but let me get it out first." In most 'normal' business meetings this would be followed with *Is that alright with everyone?* but this was no normal business. He stood up, laid both hands flat on the table, allowed his head to drop very deep and then swiftly lifted it up again and looked into everyone's eyes, one by one.

"You, little lady, have thoroughly pissed me off and you can consider yourself lucky you are still breathing and in one piece. You most certainly would not have been a few years ago and do you know what? That fact hit me last night. Why are you still walking about?" He stopped and a look that was hard to read spread across his face, with his eyebrows down and close together, his mouth was slightly open, and his nose was wrinkled. He sucked his lips into his mouth, stretched his head back, swallowed hard, released his lips and then he looked almost....... sad. Perhaps, vulnerable even.

"Two old boys and one young girl have, without even knowing it, knocked me out of my stride somewhat. PD......" He breathed hard again, he was not finding this easy.

"PD, was not one of my best decisions. I have been defending what happened, because that is what I do, but it was a bad one. I intended to get a message to you and of all the options I had to get you in line, he seemed the best. Even if he was being a prat, I was hardly going to go after my own son. Dog was always going to be a put down job and I do not agree those lightly, which is lucky for him as he was testing me. Anti to common folklore, I do not approve hidings to innocent children, let alone killing them. But there is always a risk with these things. Those dosey bastards made a hash of it. I have put on a brave face and played up to it, but inside I was not proud of that selection." His large palm covered his mouth and he slowly dragged it across his face.

"Then there is Stoney. He has been gobbing off a bit, so I thought I would show him, and everyone he had been gassing to, who was the boss. To prove to myself I still had 'it', I paid him a visit last night. Following our little chat, he needed hospital treatment for a knife through the hand and he will not be walking that well for a while. I had him pinned to his kitchen cabinet and could have kicked the absolute shit out of him, but I didn't. That man has known me for 20 plus years, toed the line, been a good servant when called on and because my two sons fuck up, I have to deal with him. He could have lost a tidy sum that night and was right to be pissed off. That is even without you banging his old lady, Dean. Back in the day, I would have carried on that beating with fists, clubs, iron bars and anything else I could lay my hands on. I would have sent out a message to anyone and everyone that it does not matter who is right, you just do not do anything to undermine or upset me. However, last night, I let him off. I know he still got a bit of a thrashing, but nothing to what he could have suffered. As I walked out of his house, I was questioning myself and had one voice telling me to go back in and another telling me I was right to leave. That............has never happened to me."

He turned and stared out of the window for a minute, his arms were hanging down and he was tightening and releasing his fists. Dean spoke;
"Dad, do you.........." Russ raised his right hand to the side of his head in a clear indication that he did not want to be interrupted.
"Thank you Dean, but let me continue in my own good time." The hand went down. He came around the front of the desk and sat on the edge of it.
"Then Carly, out there, let slip that she felt I was 'stressed' a lot of late and that she missed having you around, Rich, and Chan. Know what? So do I. It was just I did not realise it until she said it or perhaps I was being pig-headed like normal. Yes, I do know it is something I am susceptible to." Should they laugh or deny this, it was hard to know.
"So, here we are, and you are wondering what will come next. Doing what I do has taken a toll on me that I had not realised. I have blocked out those voices in my head that may have made me question what I was doing, but the circumstances of late have made me reflect; Rich, PD, Stoney, Chan, Carly and who knows what else." He seemed distant, looking up as he said those names, possibly recalling the events he

had mentioned. Then he snapped out of it.
"Upshot is, I will be taking a break and Dean I want you to run things for me." Dean looked shocked and he shook his head a tiny bit. "Don't worry, I will make sure you have some good people around you and it might not be for long; I really do not know." Rich shuffled in his chair and once he had his father's attention he asked,
"What will you do dad?"
"Sweet Fanny Adams I hope. I have money, it's a big world and I am going to see some or all of it. As for you, I do not want you in the business. I'm not being a dick about this and it is not retribution or anything like that. There can only be one guvnor and of the two of you, he is far more likely to keep the ship steady in my absence. You wanted out, you got it."
"And Donna?"
"Ah yes, Donna. I doubt we will ever be the best of friends. Who knows the way my head is now I am sure I will move from blame, to resentment and one day I may even thank you. Fucking unlikely, but you should never say never."
"Is the business with her concluded dad, or do we keep looking over our shoulders?"
"Dean will need to decide that now. Nice little introduction to the hot seat Deano; do you favour the business over your brother's girlfriend?" The corner of his mouth rose on the right side only, he enjoyed that.
"I want to run through some stuff with Dean now. Rich, I will be in touch before I go and perhaps you, Dean and me can have a pint together before I go." Rich nodded, "Yeah, I would like that."
"As for you Donna, with the greatest respect, can you fuck off out of my office please?" Was that a joke? No-one knew, so she looked at him, then averted her eyes down and away and made a beeline for the door. Rich stood, tapped his brother on the shoulder and escorted her out.

As they moved through the reception area, Dean let go of Donna and headed for Carly. He lifted her off the seat by her shoulders and gave her a massive hug. She looked at Donna over him with a look of bewilderment and gently hugged him back. "What's all this for?" she asked in a quiet voice. He let her go and said, "I have missed you too." They walked to his car in silence, where Dog was propping himself up against a wall next to it. He did not look happy.
"Well?" he said.
"I will try and explain when we get home, but in summary, Russ wants a holiday, Dean's in charge and Rich needs a new job."
"What about you?"
"It's all a bit muddy, but I think we are off the hook. That right Rich?"
"Yep. I will sort things with Dean. Fuck me, it's over."

CHAPTER 34.

It's not how big the house is, it's how happy the home is. - Unknown.

Chan was watching some TV when the phone rang, he paused the show and picked up his mobile;
"Hello,"
"Chan, it's Dean."
"Hey man, what's happening?"
"I have a proposal to make to you, can we talk?"
"Look, I do not want anything to do with...."
"Hear me out and then decide," Dean interrupted.
"I think you are wasting your time."
"And I think I am outside and would like to tell you what I am proposing. There will be no hard feelings if you say no."
"You are outside? Now?"
"Yeah."
"If this is some trick by your dad, I will break you in half. Now, do you still want to come in."
"I am not here for my dad, I am here for me. No tricks."
"Come on in then." He got up and opened his door to see Dean striding towards him; they fist bumped and Chan ushered him into the living room and offered him a seat.
"How have you been Chan?"
"I'm good. Got a couple of calls from guys interested in me working for them, but as Russ is the boss of these streets there is nothing local, so I am weighing up my options at present."
"Let me cut to the chase. Dad is taking a break from the firm for a while, please do not ask me why or for how long, because I am not sure why and I have no idea for how long." Chan sat upright, his body language evidencing his curiosity.
"What the...."
"I know. It took us all by surprise. Anyway, what that means is I am running the shop whilst he is away, and I need the best people around me I can get. You know the business, you can make sure I do not do anything stupid and everyone knows you, so anyone seeing this as a chance to move in will think twice."
"I have a question. How the hell do you expect me to stop you doing anything stupid?" They smiled.
"The break from work has done nothing for your humour. So, what do you think?

You would not have to learn a new patch or work for a new firm. What you do when, and if, dad comes back is up to you. This is working for me, right now."
"Dean, it says a lot that you came here today, so I will think it over and give you a shout tomorrow. Where does Rich fit into all this?"
Dean then spent the next 10 minutes getting Chan up to date on all that been happening. Then he left, and he shook Chan by the hand, "I could really do with you back in the business, I hope you can see your way clear to coming back." Chan said nothing, but just gave a tiny nod of his huge head and then closed the door behind him.

* * *

Rav was on his way in to see Russ for their regular chat about how the finances were and what he suggested Russ did to maximise profit and minimise cost. They had some new offers to launder money that he felt they should discuss. Each new deal of this sort carried its own risks; was it a sting by one or other law enforcement outfit, were these the type of people to crawl into bed with and was the gain worth the risk? He had done his homework and was ready to brief Russ.

As he entered the room he saw Dean was there too and that was not the norm. He acknowledged him and then looked away.
"Morning Boss."
"Good morning Rav," said with real enthusiasm and in a loud voice. "I guess you are wondering why Dean is here today?"
"Not really."
"No? Well let me enlighten you anyway." Fingers steepled as always and rocking in his chair very slightly.
"I would like to give you a pay rise." Rav looked at Russ, then to Dean and back to Russ. He began to beam, which is just what Russ was waiting for.
"I would like to, but as you have been giving yourself a nice little bonus on a regular basis anyway, I am not sure if it would be right to give you even more of my money." Straight to it as always. Fingers still tightly pressed against each other, he allowed the chair to bring him upright. He was glaring at Rav. In situations like this he did not do blinking.
"Boss, I......"
"There is a danger that a part of you wants to deny it, but that would be really silly and annoy me. Do you want to annoy me Rav?"
"No Boss." His voice was shaky. How much does he know about?
"Good. You now have a couple of options, well three actually, but I'm assuming that you do not want to die. Am I correct in that?" Rav did not say anything, the game was up and now he was going to have to play along with this performance. He rested

his elbows on his legs and covered his face with his hands. Russ knew he had him.
"Rav? Am I correct in that?" Rav moved his head to indicate he would choose a life in the pocket of Russ as opposed to death.
"Wise choice. So, you can either pay me back all the money you have stolen, with of course an extortionate rate of interest added on, or you can pay me off by carrying on doing the books, but knowing you will still need to pay me back."
"Boss, I just.........."
"Save it. Dean here wants at least a leg broken and if you try to find an excuse for what you have done I might let him get his way. You thought you were too smart for me, but I have been on to you for ages. It goes without saying that if you make a run for it I will have you hunted down, dragged back and after a serious reorganisation of your facial figures I will triple your debt. Cut the bollocks, can you pay me straight out?"
"No."
"Then you now work for Dean. He is head of the business for the time being and you will be a good servant to him or he will chop your balls off. I want you to show Carly what you do and she will gradually take over from you. Do a good job and when I let you go I might forego the hiding I so want to give you right now." He stood up, came around the desk and lifted Rav off his seat by his jacket lapels, staring deeply into the terrified, tear filled eyes in front of him. He kept up this stare, moving his vision from one scared eye to the other, and then, as Rav began to wonder what was going to happen next, he lifted his knee hard into Rav's testicles. He doubled over and Russ let go of the jacket, watching him fall to the floor coughing, wheezing and holding his balls instinctively.
"Now get out and tomorrow you come and see Dean so he can hear how you plan to pay me back. You might not think it right now, but today is your lucky day, because I have killed people for less." Dean got out of his seat and grabbed Rav by his collar and half dragged him to the door. He opened it and threw Rav into the corridor with a hefty kick up the backside to help him on his way.

"Dad, do you really think we should trust him?"
"Don't be stupid Dean, of course you cannot trust him. However, you tell me who you can trust to do your books? He is in our debt and he is scared shitless right now, which I think makes him pretty likely to behave himself, don't you? We'll get Carly trained up and decide about him in time, but for now keep him on a short rope."

* * *

Donna was mixing up her work out. Having just finished on the speed ball, she was moving on to the heavy bag, when a hush descended in the gym. Chan had walked in. Not his usual entrance ahead of Russ though. He looked calm, as unthreatening

as he could, and he asked where Tommy was. The lad pointed at the office and Chan made his way there. Donna carried on thumping the bag. As she paused for breath she saw Tommy was heading towards her, "Can I see you in the office Donna?" She looked down the gym and could only see the back of Chan's head. "Why? What does he want?" Tommy was already on his way back, "Come and find out." Then he shouted over his shoulder, "And be cool; OK?" Tommy held the door for Donna and then shut it behind him, so they could have the merest resemblance of privacy a flimsy door provides.
"No need for introductions, so let's get to it. Chan has something to say and he would like you to hear it. Chan."

Chan stroked his chin with a massive hand.
"Dean wants me to work for him and I think I can get him to invest some money in the gym as part of me agreeing."
"Tommy, this is your call. Why am I involved?"

Chan spoke, before Tommy had a chance to say anything. "You were close to PD and you are close to Rich. To keep the gym going would be what PD wanted and it will help if Rich is on board to influence Dean. That is why."
Tommy jumped in, "I would like to have your view Donna. We are two of the old guard here and obviously you and PD were super close."
"My view is we cannot be beholding to these fuckers. They will demand a 'return' or use us in some way. They killed PD, don't forget." Chan sat forward.
"Do not include me in your 'they'. Russ did that, and now he is out of the picture. Dean will put the money in as part of my package for returning; no repayment, no expectations of favours. Tommy can run the gym full time and give up his job and I will be in the background as and when he needs me."
"Conscience money is it?"
"Not from me. All I know is the future of this gym can be sorted and we both know that would have been important to PD. The money can pay Tommy and perhaps provide some new equipment."
"Why? Why are you doing this?"
"I liked PD, really liked him, and this neighbourhood is better with a boxing gym than without it. It is my neighbourhood too. The kids need somewhere to go and in Tommy we have a good guy who they will listen to. I have decided I will work for Dean, so if you want me to make this part of it, let me know later today." He held on to the sides of the chair and heaved his massive frame out of it. As he departed he gave Tommy a friendly dig in the stomach and then slapped him on the back as he moved through the door. Tommy looked at Donna, "What happened to playing it cool? So, what do you think?" She put her hands on her hips.
"Absolute no brainer. We are all in their pockets anyway, as I found out, so we might as well have some cash out of it. I am really pleased you get to take over from PD, Tommy. As your first job can you find me a decent coach?" The pleasure on his face at her first comment was replaced with surprise as he registered the second one.

"You cheeky cow."
"I will speak to Rich and make sure he has a good word with Dean for you. Isn't it funny, out of all this shit the gym gets a new lease of life. PD will be pissing himself.

* * *

Donna and Dog spent some time with Maggie and Sam before putting them to bed and then she sat him down, "We need to talk." He made himself comfortable in one of the single chairs, but was clearly uncomfortable as he waited for her to speak.

"Dad, are you enjoying being part of our family?"
"Loaded question, what's your point?"
"I like you being around and it is great the kids know you and get on with you so well."
"But?"
"Can you be a granddad to them, I mean a real granddad?"
"Not sure what you mean. Do you not like who I am?"
"You chose a way of life, when Helen and me were young, and we did not see very much of you. I will not allow you to become a part of their world and then disappear. Give that part of your life up for good, that is what I am asking of you. Can you?"
"I have."
"You might not be involved in street fights or the like, but I saw you with Russ the other day and I know you had already spoken to Chan and Russ."
"I am not getting this."
"Maggie and Sam are all that matters in this. I am their mum, for all intents and purposes, so I will be with them for as long as they need me. Rich and you will either play by my rules or be out of the picture. Can you do that?"
"I thought I had."
"What about if Chan and you had got into a fight? You will be all macho about it and talk about who would win, but that could mean you either get badly hurt or die. Same with when you messed with Russ; the fact is we are both fortunate to still be here and all limbs intact. That is you thinking as the man you were. I need you to be a cuddly, soppy, old granddad."
"Donna, I am who I am. I can try, and I have tried, but if anything threatens those kids then I cannot say I will not want to sort out whoever is upsetting them."
"Who will be the man of the house?"
"Rich."
"Rich will wear the trousers yes, and you will accept that. But I will say what does and does not happen with those kids. If you want to be involved on anything dodgy then clear out now. If not, and you can accept what I have just said, then it will be great for Sam to have you and Rich in his life."

"I will not do anything daft I promise. That is as good as I can say, but I love being around you and the kids."
"We agree then. First things first; the kids call you grandad and never Dog and you correct them if they do."
"Why?"
"Because at some point you would need to explain where that horrible name came from. Grandad Ralph it is."
"Come on Donna, no-one calls me Ralph."
"Then it's time they did. All part of being a full on grown up dad. Sorry, Grandad. I mean Grandad Ralph."
"OK, but you're making a big mistake. They would be the coolest kids on the playground with a Grandad called Dog."
"Which means, you don't think they are the coolest kids now."
"Why do women twist everything we say. I give in, have it your way."

* * *

Rich and Donna were enjoying making plans and as part of this they discussed moving in together, in a new place far better to bring kids up in. Rich had suggested he take them all out for a meal and then they could discuss him being the boyfriend and all that stuff. Donna got them ready and just before they left she explained they were going to meet a man she liked, they had seen him before and he wanted to get to know them better. They would walk to the Pizza restaurant and meet him there.

Maggie and Sam had obviously come up when Rich and Donna were talking about their relationship and especially the big step of moving in together. He knew, and she made it clear, that either he accepted them or the whole thing was off. "I know stuff all about kids, but I know how I feel about you." She did not look overly impressed with what he thought was a brilliant thing to say. "Rich, I will not allow any more upset in their life, so I have to know you are in it for the long haul. Otherwise they get used to having a man about, and then you leave a hole and more crap to deal with. When I said 'man', that's you by the way." He put his hands on her forearms and slid them down to her wrists, "Your dad is a nutter, you are not much better, you live in a rented flat and I have always known that the kids come with you. Yet, I am still here and more keen than ever to be with you. What more do you want?" She went to throw her arms around him, but realised he was holding her wrists tight and she could not move them. "Before I let you go, promise me there will be no punching for calling you crazy." She softened her arms, "Of course not!" He let go and she thumped him on the upper arm. "Hey! You said there would be no punching." Then she hugged him. "I said there wouldn't be for calling me crazy; that was for calling my dad a nutter." He hugged her back.

"Sneaky."
"I know."

Rich said hello to both of them, gave Donna a peck on the cheek and they all sat down. Sam was staring at him;
"Can I ask you something?"
"Of course."
"Are you Rich?"
"Yes. My name is actually Richard, but everyone calls me Rich. You have seen me before though."
"I know, I said are you rich?" and then he rubbed his thumb and forefinger together.

Printed in Great Britain
by Amazon